Gordon Stables, Harrison Weir

Shireen and her Friends

Pages from the life of a persian cat

Gordon Stables, Harrison Weir

Shireen and her Friends
Pages from the life of a persian cat

ISBN/EAN: 9783337288815

Printed in Europe, USA, Canada, Australia, Japan

Cover: Foto ©Andreas Hilbeck / pixelio.de

More available books at **www.hansebooks.com**

SHIREEN AND HER FRIENDS

Pages from the Life of a Persian Cat

BY

GORDON-STABLES, M.D., C.M.

(Surgeon Royal Navy)

Author of "Sable and White," "Leaves from the Log of a Gentleman Gipsy," &c., &c.

ILLUSTRATED BY HARRISON WEIR

"Thou dear little friend, and soft,
Breathing a gentle air of hearth and home,
Whose low purr to the lonely ear doth oft,
With deep refreshment come."

LONDON

JARROLD AND SONS, 10 & 11, WARWICK LANE, E.C.

[All Rights Reserved]

1895

Dedication.

TO

A. C. SWINBURNE, Esq.,

THE POET,

THIS BOOK IS DEDICATED,

WITH EVERY FRIENDLY WISH AND FEELING,

BY

THE AUTHOR.

MY LITTLE PREFACE.

(Dedicated to the Reviewer.)

Yes, this little preface is written for the Reviewer and nobody else. Indeed, the public seldom bother to read prefaces, and small blame to them. Reading the preface to a book is just like being button-holed by some loquacious fellow, as you are entering the theatre, who wants to tell you all about the play you are just going to see. So sure am I of this, that I had at first thought of writing my preface in ancient Greek. Of course every reviewer is as well-versed in that beautiful language as Professor Geddes, or John Stuart Blackie himself. I was only restrained by remembering that my own Greek might have got just a trifle mouldy.

Well, all I want to say in this page is, that there is a deal more truth in the pages that follow than might at first be imagined.

Both Shireen and Tom Brandy were real characters, and the incidents and adventures of their life on board ship were very much as I have told them. The starling, and Cockie, the cockatoo, were also pets of my own ; and Chammy, the chameleon, is described from the life. She died this year (1894).

The story Stamboul tells about his life as a show cat is a sad one, and alas ! it tells but half the truth. Cat shows have done good to the breed of cats in this country, but it has raised up a swarm of dealers, that treat poor pussy in a shameful way, and look upon her as simply so much merchandise.

In conclusion, I am not going to deny, that while trying to write a pleasant book as a companion to my last year's "Sable and White," I have endeavoured now and then to get a little hint slipped in edgeways, which, if taken by the intelligent reader, may aid in gaining a more comfortable position in our homesteads for our mutual friend the cat. If I be successful in this, I shall consider myself quite as good as that other fellow, you know, who caused two blades of grass to grow where only one grew before.

GORDON-STABLES.

The Jungle,
 Twyford,
  Berks.

SWINBURNE AND THE CAT.

The following beautiful verses by the poet Swinburne, to whom I have the honour of dedicating this work, appeared last year in the "Athenæum."

TO A CAT.

STATELY, kindly, lordly friend,
    Condescend
Here to sit by me, and turn
Glorious eyes that smile and burn,
Golden eyes, love's lustrous meed,
On the golden page I read.

All your wondrous wealth of hair,
    Dark and fair,
Silken-shaggy, soft and bright
As the clouds and beams of night,
Pays my reverent hand's caress
Back with friendlier gentleness.

Dogs may fawn on all and some
    As they come ;
You, a friend of loftier mind,
Answer friends alone in kind.
Just your foot upon my hand
Softly bids it understand.

Morning round this silent sweet
    Garden-seat
Sheds its wealth of gathering light,
Thrills the gradual clouds with might,
Changes woodland, orchard, heath,
Lawn and garden there beneath.

Fair and dim they gleamed below :
    Now they glow
Deep as even your sunbright eyes,
Fair as even the wakening skies.
Can it not or can it be
Now that you give thanks to see?

May not you rejoice as I,
    Seeing the sky
Change to heaven revealed, and bid
Earth reveal the heaven it hid
All night long from stars and moon,
Now the sun sets all in tune?

What within you wakes with day
    Who can say?
All too little may we tell,
Friends who like each other well,
What might haply, if we might,
Bid us read our lives aright.

                A. C. SWINBURNE.

CONTENTS.

SHIREEN & HER FRIENDS.

CHAPTER I

"YOU'RE THE NEW DOG, AREN'T YOU?"

 I was an autumn evening, or rather afternoon, for the sun was still high over the blue hills of the West. The sky was clear too, and twilight would last long.

The trees, however, were already casting longer shadows on the grass, and the breeze that swayed their branches, cast, playfully, ever and anon, handfuls of brown leaves towards the earth.

Shireen was coming slowly across the road towards Uncle Ben's bungalow.

Uncle Ben was an old sea captain, and had been in India for some years of his life. This was the reason why he called his home a bungalow. It really was a sturdy stone-built cottage, a verandah in front to which in June and July the roses clung, with two gables embowered in the greenery of ivy, one of which had a large casement window in it, with steps leading down to the lawn, where, under the trees in the sweet summer-time Ben was often to be found smoking a pipe in his grass hammock.

The whole place was a sort of arboretum, however, and the very most the sun could ever do was to shine down upon the grass in patches. Once inside the railing that surrounded it Shireen knew she would be safe, so there was no need to hurry. Besides, it had been raining, and the road was not only wet, but the water lay here and there in little pools.

These pools Shireen took care to avoid, for she was a very dainty cat indeed. Every time she took a step she lifted her paw as high as she could and shook it. She tried also to elevate that tail of hers so as to keep it unsoiled, but it was so big and bushy that in this she was only partially successful.

The bungalow lay or stood in the outskirts or suburbs of the village, and not a long way from the sea either, for old Ben would have slept but poorly could he not have gone to sleep every night—that is every still night—with the whisper of the waves singing a kind of lullaby to him as they broke lazily on the yellow sands. But if a breeze blew off the shore or down from the hills to the nor'ard and east, then Ben went to sleep with the half-formed idea in his mind that he was at sea; an idea that ere long commingled with his dreams. The wind would seem to be roaring through rigging and shrouds, and not through the oaks and elms and rustling pine trees; but sail was shortened, the ship was snug, and it was the mate's watch on deck. What more could any sailor desire?

Ben had no wife; only a little old woman came and

chared for him, and a tall ungainly Portuguese lad, who
had been cook's mate with him on board the *Alibi*, and
could make an excellent curry, officiated as Ben's factotum
and valet. Then there was the cockatoo. Perhaps it
may be said that cockatoos don't count as members of a
household, but Cockie was no ordinary cockatoo, I can
assure you. She came originally from the bush or jungle
of Western Australia. Ben used to nod his head at
Cockie in a semi-solemn kind of way when anyone put a
question to him concerning the bird.

She came into my possession in a queer kind of way.
Some of these days I may tell you the story. Haven't
told it to anybody yet except to Pussy Shireen. Some
day?—Yes, some day—perhaps.

The little old woman who chared for Ben only came
once a week, and that was on a Friday. Then Ben would
clear out, get away to the hills, or off in a boat, with bread
and cheese in his coat-tail pocket, and not come home till
evening.

Fridays were called by this sailor "wash-and-scrub-deck-
days," and there wasn't a deal of comfort in them. Besides,
Ben dreaded a woman's tongue.

"And old Sally's tongue," he would tell his friends, " is
about the waggingest thing out. Just set the old creature
agoing, and she'll go on without a hitch for a two hours'
spell as steady's the trade wind."

So he was always glad when Sally finished her tea in
the kitchen, received her well-earned two shillings, and
took her departure. Then, and not until then, would
Ben sink into his rocking-chair with a sigh of relief
and satisfaction, and light his very largest meerschaum
pipe.

Ben never boasted about Sally, but he was willing enough to talk about Pedro, or the cockatoo.

"He is a faithful creature, a faithful creature, and I don't care who knows it. And the curry he makes! Ah!" It will be noted that Ben would be alluding thus to Pedro, not to Cockie the cockatoo. "Yes, that curry, why, the very flavour of it takes ten years off my life at least. Calls me as regular of a morning as a bo's'n's pipe. Eight bells, and there I am; clothes all brushed and folded; bath waiting for me; clean white shirt laid out, and never a button missing off my waistcoat. Breakfast served nice and comfortable soon's I go down; letters alongside my plate, and Cockie's cage as sweet as nuts. A faithful creature indeed, although he isn't much to look at!"

No. Ben spoke the truth, for certainly Pedro was not much to look at; not much to admire. He wore the same dress apparently winter and summer; a very short blue-cloth sailor's jacket, under this a checked shirt, no necktie, no collar, no waistcoat. The continuations of his dress downwards did not reach to his low-heeled shoes by inches, so he always showed a goodly amount of blue-ribbed stocking. But his shoes were always nicely polished, and his long lean hands were clean. In complexion Pedro was sallow, almost saffron-hued, and his eyes were like this jet; while his hair, which was black, of course, was scarcely half-an-inch long all over, and stood on end like the bristles of a blacking brush. People used to say that at some period of his life Pedro must have seen a ghost, and that his hair had never fallen flat again.

"But he is good to the birds," Ben would have told you.

"God's birds, I mean," he would have added. "The birds that cheer us and charm us in the sweet spring-time, you know, and all the summer through.

> " 'All thro' the sultry hours of June,
>   From morning blithe to golden noon,
>   And till the star of evening climbs
>   The gray-blue zest, a world too soon,
>   There sings a thrush among the limes.'

Aye, and that bird, and our blackbirds with their mellow music, and bold lilting chaffie and tender-songed cock-robin know Pedro, and when the winter snows are on the lawn they will almost feed out of his hand. They know me, too, and they know Cockie, and they know Colonel Clarkson's cat Shireen."

And that, reader, is the very cat that is now slowly and wearily crossing the road towards the good old sailor's bungalow. Shireen, it will therefore be observed, did not belong to Ben. She was simply an occasional visitor, for cats very soon find out who loves them and who does not.

But Ben's bungalow was not the only place to which Shireen was in the habit of paying a visit. No, not by very many. Indeed, everybody knew Shireen, and there were few houses in the village that this strange cat did not walk into now and then. Very coolly, too; but always with a little fond cry or expression of friendliness and goodwill to the inmates.

She was always welcome, and many a saucerful of creamy milk was put down to her on these occasions. Not that Shireen paid the visit for sake of being fed, for often she would not touch the milk-offering. But she had formed this wandering habit somehow. The fact is, Shireen,

B

like her owner, the Colonel, was a very far-travelling cat, and cats, like old soldiers and old sailors who have been here and there in many lands, find it difficult to settle in one place or one home.

If ever a cat was a village favourite, this droll puss Shireen was.

It must not be supposed, however, that she was anybody's cat, for a cupful of milk, as the saying is. For there were people that Shireen liked better than others, and some she did not like at all; while there were men and women that she would fly from, and houses in the village that she gave a wide berth to.

Sometimes she would take it into her head to pay a visit to the girls' school during working hours. The young lady teachers did not object, because she did not interfere with the duties; but here again she evinced likes and dislikes. Pretty Matty Loraine, for example, she quietly ignored, and never responded to her caresses, but to everybody's astonishment she seemed greatly attached to Emily Stoddart, although Emily was considered somewhat plain in appearance, and not very clever. Besides, she had red hair; but she had soft blue eyes, and perhaps Shireen had found out down in their hidden depths a gentle nature dwelt.

Everybody said that when Matty grew up she would be very beautiful indeed, and might possibly marry the squire's son, but a wealthy marriage was never prophesied for poor Emily. There were stonemasons and hedgers or ditchers for girls like her. However, prophecies did not seem to trouble Emily, though the evident preference that Shireen showed for her pleased her not a little. Perhaps cats are students of human character, and in very truth they need to be if they are to enjoy life at all, and give themselves a chance of securing the allotted span of eighteen or twenty years which Providence has decreed as the extent of poor persecuted pussy's existence—in this world at all events.

Singularly enough, Shireen evinced not the slightest fear of dogs. As a rule, I mean, though every rule has its exceptions. But puss could have told you the idiosyncrasies of all the dogs in the village downwards, from the doctor's great good-natured Newfoundland, on whose broad back all the children in the place had ridden when very young. *He* wouldn't touch a cat. He was too noble by far. Nor would the saddler's bull-dog, ferocious-looking and ugly to a degree though he was ; nor Squire Blythe's mastiff ; nor Miss Ponsonby's collie, with his long shaggy coat, his beautiful face and gentle eyes.

Whenever a new dog came to the village Shireen set out to meet him and make friends with him. She would come trotting up to the fresh arrival with her tail in the air, and purring nearly as loud as a turtle dove, and some such conversation as the following might be supposed to take place between the two.

SHIREEN *(loquitur)*: "Oh, you're the new dog, aren't you ? What's your name, and what's your breed ? I'm simply delighted to see a new face ! "

FRESH ARRIVAL *(looking astonished)*: "My name is Cracker. My breed is the Airdale terrier. I come from Yorkshire. I have fought and slain an otter single-handed. I'm a terrible fellow when I'm put out. My duty is to kill rats, and—listen—sometimes even *cats.*"

SHIREEN *(purring louder than ever)*: "Oh, I daresay and, indeed, Cracker, some cats deserve to be killed. But I'm Shireen. Nobody ever kills me. What a nice good-natured face you have! Just let me rub my back against your chest. So—and—so! I'm sure we shall be tremendous friends, and you might do me a favour if you care to."

FRESH ARRIVAL: " Is it rats?"

SHIREEN: " No, it isn't rats. It is Danger, the butcher's bull-terrier. He wants killing ever so much. He thinks he can fight any dog, and he always chases me. But be sure you shake him well up whenever you meet him. He has one ear slit in two. I managed that for him one day. I'll sit in a tree and see you open him up, and nobody will be a bit sorry. Good-bye, you beautiful handsome Cracker. So pleased to have met you. Just over the way there, in that low-thatched cottage, there is a sick child, and I am going in to sit and sing to her till she drops off asleep and forgets her pains and sorrows. Good-bye."

Shireen, it will be seen, quite disarmed dogs by her coolness and her perfect friendliness. No dog that ever lived would kill a cat who ran up to meet him in the street and rubbed her head against his chest.

This strange pussy had, however, one or two human enemies as well as the dog Danger. Almost everyone has, and Shireen could be no exception. But in her case they were either old wives, who looked upon her with superstitious dread because she was reported to carry a ruby in one of her teeth, or they were mischievous boys, who threw stones at her from that nasty little contrivance called a catapult, or cat-a-*pelt*, as some horrid boys call it, because they think it was invented to pelt poor pussies with.

Shireen, however, had managed hitherto to keep out of their way. She was very often to be seen in the village street, walking along leisurely enough, but as soon as that

hideous yell was borne along on the breeze, which told her
the boys' school had just been dismissed, pussy increased
her pace and disappeared.

Shireen knew boys. She knew all their tricks and
their manners, and she could have told you that boys were
boys all the wide world over.

Well, as she is crossing the street to-day, giving a glance
up and down every two or three seconds to make certain
the coast was clear, the rattle of light wheels was heard.

That was the butcher's cart.

She listened and looked, one paw in the air.

Yes, there was Danger himself coming round the corner
with his red tongue lolling out of his open mouth, for
though it was autumn the weather was warm.

Danger sees pussy almost as soon as she sees him.

" There's that long-tailed white cat again," he says to
himself. " Well, I'll have her this time right enough.
Here goes ! "

And straight along the road he comes rushing with the
speed of a torpedo.

Shireen doesn't lose her presence of mind. Not a bit of
it. She measures the distance with a glance from Uncle
Ben's railing, and calculates to the tenth part of a second
the time it will take her to reach it.

She wants to make that dog believe that he is sure of her,
so that she may, in triumph and safety, enjoy his chagrin
and disappointment all the more.

On he comes, on and on.

Shireen pretends she doesn't see him.

He is within two yards of her. Oh ! he has caught her !
No, he hasn't ! One dart, one dive, and she is safe on the
other side of Ben's friendly railing.

He—Danger—can't get through.

Only just his nose, and no more.

And what a fool he was to stick that between the rails. Shireen springs round like fire from flint.

"Fuss! Fut!"

That blow was beautifully aimed, and poor Danger goes howling off with a sadly torn nose.

I say *poor* Danger, because it really was the fault of that wicked butcher-boy. Dogs are only what men make them.

Shireen is not so young as she was once upon a time, but she feels very youthful now. And very happy too. She stops for a few minutes to dry herself in a patch of sunshine, then goes galloping off across Ben's lawn, making pretences that the withered leaves are mice, and whacking them about in all directions.

Next moment she has jumped into Ben's hammock.

"Why, old girl," cries Ben, "you're as playful as a kitten. Who would think, Shireen, that you were over twenty years of age, and had seen nearly as much of the world as Uncle Ben himself? Well, sit there and sing to me. Now, that is real soothing, and I'm not at all sure I won't go to sleep. For at my time of life, Shireen, it's best to take all out of life you can get."

Ben's hand and book drop listlessly on his breast, and while the autumn wind goes moaning through the pine trees overhead, keeping up a kind of sibilant bass to Shireen's song, while his pet cockatoo nods on his perch near by, the ancient mariner doses—and dreams.

CHAPTER II.

" The day is done, and the darkness
Falls from the wings of night,
As a feather is wafted downward
From an eagle in its flight ;

" But the night shall be filled with music,
And the cares that infest the day,
Shall fold their tents, like the Arabs,
And as silently steal away."

O cares had Colonel Clarkson to trouble him. So everyone would have told round the village or in the parish. It was then nearly the autumn of life with the Colonel, but really and truly he seemed to be growing old gracefully. Nor did he allow the little worries of life to interfere in the least with the calm enjoyment of his placid existence.

He had been a busy man in his younger days. But that was years ago. He had fought in the Crimea, he had waved his sword on Persian plains, and on Afghanistan heights, and he had gone through all the horrors of the Indian Mutiny. He had even been side by side with

brave Havelock in the rush for the Residency up that long
street of death and fire where brave Neill fell.   Yet concerning these and his many other adventures he was
seldom very communicative, albeit there were times when
his friend Uncle Ben succeeded in drawing him out, and
then his stories were well worth listening to.

The Colonel was like many brave soldiers, a somewhat
shy man, and certainly kept himself personally very much
in the background when describing a battle or the storm-
ing of a trench against fearful odds.   That he had not
kept himself in the background on the real field of fight
was evident enough from the medals he had won but
seldom if ever wore.   And one of these was the Victoria
Cross.

When the Colonel did suffer himself to be drawn out, as
Sailor Ben phrased it, he never told his stories excitedly,
but in low calm tones, and in earnest conversational
English, that carried conviction of the truthfulness of every
item of his narrative to the hearts of his listeners.

And who would these listeners be?   I must tell you
that, and having done so I shall have introduced you to
most of the personalities who figure in this biography.

The listeners then may, indeed they must be, divided
into two groups   The first group was composed of human
beings, the second of what I am loth indeed to call the lower
animals.   It is mere conventionality on my part to do so,
for the creatures God has permitted us to domesticate, and
who are such faithful and trustworthy servants, are often-
times quite as interesting in a way as many of their
masters—men.

*   *   *

On that very autumnal evening on which Shireen paid her visit to Uncle Ben's bungalow, and made it so hot for the butcher's dog, our two groups were all together around the fire at the Colonel's Castle, as the old soldier's house was generally called, and Castle it once had been in reality.

On this particular evening after Ben had finished his pipe and drank the tea that Pedro had brought him, he had smoothed pussy once more, and said :—" I think now, Shireen, we'll take a walk to the Castle and see your master. By that time gloaming will be falling, and it will be what my dear friend the Colonel calls the 'Children's Hour.'"

"Meow!" said puss, as if she knew all about it, and quite understood every word that Uncle Ben said when he repeated Longfellow's dreamy lines :

> " Between the dark and the daylight,
> When the night is beginning to lower,
> Comes a pause in the day's occupations,
> That is known as the Children's Hour.

> " I hear in the chamber above me
> The patter of little feet,
> The sound of a door that is opened,
> And voices soft and sweet."

People who had met Uncle Ben this evening walking along towards the Colonel's Castle, were not a bit astonished to see Shireen trotting contentedly beside him, her tail in the air and head erect ; nor to see his wonderful cockatoo balancing himself uneasily on his shoulder, and giving vent now and then to a war-whoop that would have scared a Comanche Indian, and certainly frightened the dogs.

Uncle Ben's cockatoo was as often on his shoulder as anywhere else, and the bird was a frequent visitor at the old Castle, only he insisted on remaining on his master's shoulder all the time he stayed there, generally taking stock of things around him ; sometimes making a remark or two of his own, or allaying his feelings with a little dance or a song.

Well, Ben was one of Colonel Clarkson's listeners to-night. But there were three others, namely, the Colonel's wife, a lady who was still strangely interestingly-pleasing to behold, although she was evidently not English. People called her beautiful. She must have been many years younger than her husband, all owing to the fact that women age sooner than men. On the swaying, sighing trees outside yonder, the leaves had assumed their autumn tints. There were autumn tints on Colonel Clarkson's hair as well, but the tints on both were beautiful. Tom, a handsome boy of some eight years of age, sat on his aunt's knee, his head nestling on her shoulder, but his eyes on his soldier uncle. On this uncle's knee sat a fairy fragile little maiden, the boy's sister, and some two years his senior. They were orphans, and the Castle was now their home. These then were the human group.

The other group were altogether on the skin hearthrug in front of the fire—a group of undergraduates let me term them.

The members of this group were far indeed from uninteresting, each in his or her own way. But their individualisms must develop themselves as the story goes on, only I want you to be introduced to them here at once.

Shireen you already know. She is seated on a foot-

stool, singing low to herself, and gazing somewhat pensively into the fire.

She is not the only cat in the group, however. There is
a much younger one stretched on the rug. A short-haired
tabby.

And seated on top of her, busily preening his feathers
very much to his own satisfaction, is Dick. Now Dick is
a starling, and it may surprise some to learn that he is on
terms the most friendly with both cats, and that far from
seeking to harm him, they would at any hour of the day
risk their lives in protecting him.

The particular trait in Dick's character, judging from
his every look and movement, is consummate *chic* and
independence.

But there are two dogs here also, both characters in
their way.

One is a white Pomeranian. He is sitting as near as he
can get to his master's knee, for his love for Colonel
Clarkson knows neither bounds nor limits.

The other dog is the drollest, daftest, wildest little rascal
you could conceive. He is an iron-grey, hard-haired
Scotch terrier. He comes of a race of dogs that are
simply indomitable, that know no such thing as fear, who
will, single-handed, face and fight either fox, badger, or
otter, and if vanquished, know at least how to die.

There is an old-world look in that doggie's face which is
wonderful to behold, and a depth of wisdom in his dark
eyes that is unfathomable. Warlock, for that is his name,
is cheek-by-jowl with that young tabby cat, for curiously
enough, the two are inseparables. Almost every day they
go out by themselves to the fields and banks and woods,
to hunt together, and even at night they come trotting
home side by side.

So that is all my group of undergraduates—no, stay a moment. There is yet another, and in one way he or she is the drollest of the crew. In yonder far-off corner there, but not a great way from the fire, a branch of wood has been fixed in a block to keep it upright, and on one limb of this artificial tree is stretched at length a large chameleon. Chammy, as he is called, is very wide awake, and evidently enjoying the warmth of the fire, for hand after hand he extends, time about at intervals of about a minute to woo the welcome blaze.

And what a fire that is too! Pray do not let such a thing as a grate arise up before your mind's eye at my mention of the word fire. The idea of a tall ungainly grate would utterly dispel all ideas of romance.

This is a low fire, a fire of logs and coals and peat, all beautifully, artistically, and thoughtfully arranged with the art that conceals art. A fire that to sit in front of on a winter's evening would be an entertainment in itself; a fire that would make the oldest and loneliest man feel he had good company; a fire that laughs and talks to one; that speaks to the very soul itself, while it warms the very heart, and that carries the thought away back to pleasant scenes in past life, or merrily forward to a hopeful future; verily a fire to be thankful for, especially if wild winds are careering round the house, and moaning in the old-fashioned chimney, while we think of sailors far at sea.

*

Colonel Clarkson finishes his story, and stretches out his hand to find his pipe. Lizzie snuggles up closer to his chest, and pats his cheek with her fingers.

"God brought you safely back, didn't he, dearest?" she says.

Uncle Clarkson kisses her brow for answer.

Ben clears his throat and is about to speak. But he seems to think better of it, and commences to refill his pipe instead, smiling to himself as he does so.

But bold little Tom holds up his hand, and says grimly—

"Uncle Clarkson, when I'm a big big man I'll be a sodser (soldier), and tut (cut) off black men's heads by the store (score)!"

Ben laughs, but shakes a finger at Tom.

"Poor dear Cockie!" says the cockatoo, in a mournfully lugubrious tone.

"Eh? Eh?" cries the starling, briskly looking up from his perch on top of the tabby. "Eh? What is it? What d'ye say? Tsc, tsc, tsc."

Vee-Vee, the Pomeranian, changes his position and faces Shireen.

He looks at her for a minute, then leans his head on her footstool, but his eyes are still fixed upon her.

Shireen was Vee-Vee's foster mother. Six years ago he came to the Castle, being then a mere dossil of cotton wool apparently, with a black dot for a nose and two black dots for eyes, so that Lizzie called him a little snow dog. Well, the little snow dog was only a fortnight old, and it happened just then that Shireen had had kittens, the whole of which had died. No they had *not* been drowned, for Colonel Clarkson was too humane a man to think of depriving the pussy of all her family at once. But, I repeat, they died.

Then Shireen had taken pity on Vee-Vee, the little snow dog.

"You're an orphan," she said, or seemed to say, for it is all the same thing. "You're an orphan, and a miserable little mite at that ; well, I have oceans of milk, so I shall rear you if you are so inclined."

The little snow dog was so inclined, and Shireen took him over at once, and till this day, next to his dear master, Vee-Vee loved his foster mother.

"Just look," said Mrs. Clarkson, "how fondly Vee-Vee is gazing at his foster mother !"

"Oh," cried Lizzie, " I know what Vee-Vee wants. He wants her to tell him a story."

"Ah ! indeed," said Colonel Clarkson, "she well may tell her friends a story, for few cats have had a more adventurous life than she."

Shireen patted Vee-Vee on the nose with her paw, but the nails were sheathed, then she proceeded to tell her strange story.

Cats and all the lower animals, or undergraduates, have a language of their own, you know, but I have made myself master of it, and I shall try to translate what Shireen said. Only I must take a new chapter to it.

CHAPTER III.

HE story of my life? Was that what you asked me for, my little foster son? I see Warlock pricking one ear. He is going to listen too, is he?

Ah! well, my friends, my life has been a very long and a very eventful one, for I have travelled very far and seen much, and you all know I am getting old. Dick is laughing and chuckling to himself. Of course, he thinks that I am centuries old, but that is only because he himself is so young.

Chammy, the chameleon, looks down at Shireen with one of his droll eyes, while he watches a fly on the ceiling with the other. He holds up a hand, too, opening and shutting it as he remarks—

"Don't give yourself airs about your age, Shireen. Look at me. It is a hundred years yesterday since I came to life again."

"Came to life again, Chammy," says Warlock, winking to Dick. "Why, what are you telling us?"

"The truth," said the chameleon. "One thousand one hundred years ago yesterday—and it doesn't seem very

long to look back to—after a good dinner on butterflies
I retired into the hollow of a young banian tree in an
African forest to have a nap. I had dined heartily, and I
slept long, so long that the tree grew up over me. And
it grew and grew and grew for a thousand years till it
became the most wonderful tree in all the forest. But one
day it was rent in twain by a lightning flash, and—I awoke
and crawled out and found a moth and swallowed it."

"Tse, tse, tse!" said Dick.

"We can't be expected to swallow your story though,
Chammy," said Warlock.

Chammy did not reply, for the fly had come down from
the ceiling, and settling in front of the chameleon began
to wash its face.

Chammy turned both eyes in towards his nose, and
focused the fly, then his mouth slowly opened, and
presently out darted a long round tongue, more like a slug
than anything else, and the fly never finished washing its
face.

Well, as I was saying, continued Shireen, when
interrupted by our dear and excessively old friend
Chammy, I am getting on! Twenty years, you know,
children, is a long, long life for a cat, if not for a chameleon, and oh! what ups and downs I have seen in that
time!

My very earliest recollections take me back to scenes
in beautiful Persia, "the land of the lion and the sun."

"Some day," said Dick, the starling, making pretence to
bathe himself in tabby's glittering fur—"some day I
mean to fly there. None of you fellows have wings, so
you can't do that sort of thing. It would take poor old
Chammy yonder fully another thousand years to wriggle

that length. Better he should go to sleep again in an old log of wood!"

"Yes," continued Dick, while Shireen sat thoughtfully washing her face and gazing at the fire. "I shall go to Persia. I had quite a long talk the other day with the cuckoo about it. He says that Persia in the South is no end of a nice place, with flies and things to be found all throughout the winter. He says he wouldn't come here at all if it wasn't that there is less danger in this country in summer-time to his eggs, and the climate is more bracing for the mother and the young. The Mother Cuckoo, you must remember, is very delicate, and wouldn't think of rearing her own family, so she employs a nurse, or maybe three or four nurses; and the more fools they, *I* say, for accepting the situation, for they toil away all the best part of the summer, leaving their own little families to starve and never get a thank-you for their pains. But Mother Cuckoo is a knowing old bird; she finds a nest nicely hidden—it may be a robin's, it may be a tit-lark's, or a water wagtail's—and then a conversation begins at once.

"'Nice little place you've got here,' says Mother Cuckoo to the little bird, smiling all down both sides of her head as she speaks, for you know, Warlock, you couldn't make a cuckoo's mouth much bigger without cutting her head off. 'Nice little place!'

"'Yes,' says the little bird, feeling much flattered.

"'And such a cosy warm well-lined nest!'

"'Yes,' says the little bird again, 'my husband and I did that.'

"'How clever. And the nest is so well hidden!'

"'Oh, yes, that is the best of it. There are no cats about,

C

and wicked schoolboys would never think of looking here
for a nest.'

"'It isn't a very large nest!'

"'Oh, it is big enough for our little family.'

"'Let me see,' says Mother Cuckoo, 'you have three
eggs laid already. How clever of you!'

"'Yes, and I'm going to lay another.'

"'Your husband's from home to-day, isn't he?'

"'He has gone to the woods for a certain kind of beetle
that I've set my heart upon.'

"'Oh, dear!' says sly Mother Cuckoo, 'I do feel so faint;
all over of a tremble. Do, like a dear little mite, go and
find my husband. He is in the copse down by the miller's
pond. I'll sit here and keep your eggs warm till you
return.'

"But the little bird never finds Father Cuckoo, and when
she comes back, lo! old Mother Cuckoo has gone, but the
sly bird has left an egg bigger and different from any in
the nest. And that egg seems to throw a glamour over
the little bird; she feels compelled to hatch it, and to rear
the little one when it comes out to the neglect of her own
family, for the young cuckoo is such a powerful eater that
it takes both the little bird and her husband all their time
to gather insects for it and stuff them down its gaping
throat, and——"

"Now, Dick," cried Warlock, "if you're quite done we
would like to hear Shireen's story; you may fly to Persia
with the cuckoos in August if you like, and——"

"And perhaps never come home again," said Tabby;
"don't you go, Dick, don't you go."

From all I can recollect of Persia, said Shireen, it is
a very beautiful country in summer-time, although away

high up in the mountain fastnesses of the North, terrible snowstorms sometimes blow, and here dwell tribes and clans of wild Persian Highlanders that are at war with all the world.

Yet, strange to say, these wild men are kind to their cats, and pussy in these regions is looked upon as quite one of the family.

But it was not in these wilds that I first saw the light of day, or any other light, children, but far away in what my mother called the sunny South.

" Much game there, mother ? " asked Warlock, pricking both his ears.

" I'll come to that presently, Warlock, you mustn't interrupt, you know."

My very earliest recollections then, you must know, are all centred in my mother. This is only natural. Besides, my mother was very beautiful indeed. My little brother and I—we were both born at the same time—disagreed about many matters connected with domestic life and family arrangements, but we were both of the same opinion concerning mother's beauty. I was very young when I first opened my eyes, but I have only to close them again now, and mother rises up before me in all her loveliness. White were the snows that capped the jagged hills of the Zarda Koo, no snows could be whiter, but more spotless still, I thought, was the coat of my dam. Blue were the rifts between the clouds in the autumn, but bluer and brighter my mother's eyes. Then every movement she made was graceful and easy. Was it any wonder that brother and I loved her, or that we sometimes fought for the best place in her arms?

Looking back through the long vista of years, I cannot

help thinking that perhaps my mother loved my brother
better than me.   I am sure she spent more time in licking
him, but then I may be wrong, for I was restless, and would
at any time rather have romped with mother's tail than
submitted to her caresses when they took the shape of
licking my face and ears with her tongue.   Besides, brother
had a black spot on his brow, which mother thought she
would succeed in licking off.   So she would lick and lick
and lick until she fell back tired and exhausted on the
cushion of crimson silk that formed our bed.

I did not know then the value that human beings
attached to a cushion like this.   Nor the value of anything
around me.

Everything, brother and I believed, belonged to mother,
the whole universe, as far as we had yet seen it, belonged
to her, and the slaves that came softly stealing across the
thick carpets and placed mother's food before her in dishes
of solid gold and silver, were, in our opinion, if we thought
about the matter at all, only creatures of common clay that
lived and moved and had their beings merely to minister
to mother's wants and needs.

I am much wiser now, children, and I can tell you that
the splendid apartments where mother lived when we were
very young, were furnished with splendour and elegance,
unknown to this land of cloudy skies and misty rain.

That silk cushion, children, on which mother lay, was
richly embroidered with threads of gold, and tasselled with
pearls and precious stones.   The room itself was lofty, and
hung everywhere with curtains of rarest value.   Great
punkahs, moved by invisible hands, depended from the
roof, and, waving to and fro, kept us cool.   Costly vases
and musical instruments stood here and there, and couches

of pale-blue silk and silver were ranged along the walls. There was a dim religious light throughout, and from an arched window we could catch glimpses of gardens filled with lovely flowers and fruit, and watered by cool fountains that threw their snow-white spray far up against the blue of the sky. And everywhere the air was laden with the rich and rare odour of orange and citron blooms.

Then on the soft Persian carpets, I was afterwards told, my brother and I used to play with rubies as large as marbles.

"Something to eat?" said Dick, thoughtfully.

"No, Dick, a ruby is nothing to eat, but it is something held so sacred by human beings, that one such precious stone would buy all the fine things a man could use in a long, long lifetime."

Now, some weeks after brother and I opened our eyes, we learned to lap milk. It was difficult to do this at first, though we wanted to, because our eyes were not yet strong enough to judge distances, and sometimes when we thought we were licking the milk we were only lapping the air ; then when we put our heads further down our noses went into the silver saucer up to the eyes, and we thought we were drowned, and sprang up and sneezed.

While trying one day to lap some milk, we noticed that mother was singing to a very pretty human being, who sat cross-legged upon a low ottoman. Mother was singing, and she was also rubbing her head backwards and forwards against this lovely human creature's bare arm. Brother and I sat back and looked up in astonishment, although looking up made our heads so light that we nearly tumbled.

"Oh! aren't they funny, funny, funny?" cried a voice. It was that of the beautiful human being.

The words only sounded to us like rippling music then, music such as the birds in their golden cages made, and the spray of the fountain splashing down and falling into its marble basin. But mother afterwards translated the language to us.

Day after day now this human being sat there cross-legged on the ottoman, and we soon began to like her as much as mother did.

She was very young and very beautiful, her little mouth was a rosebud, her eyes were very large, but jetty black, not blue like mother's. She was dressed in robes of flowing silk of many colours, and when she walked, glittering chains of gold and precious stones jangled and rang. Beside her often stood a tall and powerful man-human, as dark as night, with fierce red eyes, white flashing teeth, and a girdle around his waist, from which hung an ugly half-moon knife. Brother and I were much afraid of this man-human. He was an ogre, and we ran backwards, raised our hair, and spat aloud at him when he came near us. But the young and lovely lady was not at all afraid of the ogre, but used to play with his knife and tease him.

Mother told us then that we must love the beautiful girl. She was our mistress and our queen.

Well, this would not have made brother and me love the queen one little bit, for we did not want any queen but mother. But the queen was so fond and so gentle, and used to smooth us so tenderly with her white and taper fingers, which were all bedecked with rings and sparkling stones, that we came to love her as much in time as mother seemed to do.

    *   *   *   *   *   *   *

One day we had an adventure that I shall never forget.

Far, in through the open window, sprang a splendid lion-looking cat, just like mother, only bigger and bolder. He advanced to where we all lay with a fond and loving cry; but mother sprang up in a rage. All her hair was raised from end to end, her back was arched, and her eyes flashed like glowing lights.

Brother and I got up and tried to follow her example, but we both tumbled over on the cushion and lay there in most inglorious attitudes.

"Mrrrak, mrr—mrr—mrrk!" That is what father said. Yes, Warlock, I must tell you at once this lion-like cat was our father.

At first mother advanced to meet him growling like a volcano, but he threw himself on his back and behaved in a fashion altogether so ridiculous, and with so many droll attitudes of blandishment, that mother finally softened, all her hair flowed backwards again, and she began to sing. Then she ran back to the cushion and picked my brother up, and, throwing herself on her back, held him high in her arms for father to admire.

"Mrr—wrr—wrr—wurruk!" cried father, and gently tapped brother on the back.

This so pleased mother that she jumped up and ran round and round the room. Then she came back and slapped father with a gloved hand. Then father slapped her and sent her flying half-way across the room. In a moment she sprang up and leapt on top of him, and the two rolled over and over on the carpet in mimic warfare, but so like a real battle was it, that for some time brother and I were very much afraid indeed.

Well, father came nearly every day after this, and he

nearly always brought a little bird, warm but dead, and perhaps, with a little spot of blood on its breast. I'm afraid it was sometimes a bulbul, or nightingale, and more than once it was a canary.

But it did not matter to mother one whit. She ate it, feathers and all, except the tail and the wings, growling awfully all the time she was devouring it. Meanwhile father stood aside and seemed so pleased that he did not know what to do with himself.

When she had finished the bird, brother and I had the wings and tail to play with, and we pretended to be mother, and growled like little wild beasts. Then mother would sit down and wash her face. As soon as she had done so she jumped merrily off the cushion and slapped father, and then the fun began.

One day father came into the room looking much more like a lion than ever, and he had something in his mouth.

He was growling, too, and I think mother was half afraid of him. But he came right up to the spot where brother and I were playing with our ruby, and placed a strange and weird-looking creature down right in front of us.

We had never seen such a little animal before. It wasn't a bird, for it had no wings, only feet, and fur as soft as mother's, but dark in colour. It lay on its side, and, dreadfully frightened though we were, brother and I both put up our backs and spat and growled most bravely.

The little vision in fur, which I now know to have been a harmless mouse, lay on its side quite paralysed with fear, but father stretched out his gloved hand and pushed it. Then it jumped up and ran away.

Oh, what a fright brother and I got when we saw that the

wild mouse was alive! And how brave we thought father was when he sprang after it and brought it back.

But we soon regained our courage, and father and mother stood aside to see us play with it. Whenever it escaped they brought it back.

At last the poor little morsel, all wet and bedraggled, stood up on its hind legs in front of father, and wagged its two wee naked hands in front of its nose. Mother told me afterwards what it was saying.

"Oh, kill me please," it pleaded. "Kill me quick and put me out of pain."

CHAPTER IV.

"YOU MUST HAVE A NAME, MY LOVELY FLOWER."

ITHERTO, continued Shireen, shifting her position on the footstool to one of greater comfort, hitherto, my children, the life of brother and myself had been all indoors. We knew of no other world than that bounded by the four walls of the room around us, and it never occurred to me to wonder where our lion-like father obtained the birds which he never forgot to bring mother daily.*

He did not come in through the curtained doorway that led out into the orangery with its fountains and its flowers, but leapt down from a window that was too high for us to reach.

---

* *A propos* of Shireen's father bringing the mother pussy the birds, I have a little anecdote to tell that is not without its humorous side. Some years ago I possessed a very large and handsome half-Persian white Tom, whom the children called Jujube. This cat, being allowed to roam the world at the freedom of his own will, formed an attachment with a neighbour's lady-cat, and married her. I was not invited to the marriage, so do not know when it took place, nor what speeches were made at the wedding-breakfast. However, in course of time, Mrs. G—'s cat was about to have kittens, and, not having any knowledge of how cats should be treated under such circumstances, she rather cruelly turned her out of doors. It happened at this time that Mrs. G— had also twenty-one young chickens. And now they began to disappear at the rate of

One day, the door leading into the garden was left open, and mother, discovering this, determined to take us out.

If I should live to be as old as Chammy yonder, my children, I shall never forget that morning. We followed mother timidly, fearfully, and on rather shaky legs I must admit, for we were not yet very strong.

And every time a leaf fell, or went fluttering past us we started and trembled, nay, I am not sure we did not even start at our own shadows in the strong sunlight.

We gathered a little more confidence at last, but everything was so new and so strange and so unaccountable that it seemed like walking in a dream. I looked up for a moment at the sun, but quickly withdrew my gaze ; then all was suddenly dark around me. I thought the earth had opened and swallowed us all up, and mewed in terror. But things soon became light once more, mother licked the top of my head, and on we went, now with more confidence.

There were birds singing here, and flitting to and fro through the spray of the gurgling fountains ; light and colour and beauty were everywhere. Then the air was strong and fresh and balmy, and, oh, so delightfully warm, that we soon felt perfectly at home, and bold enough even to chase the fluttering leaves.

But for all this we would not venture far away from

one every day, and so on for nineteen days. Her cat had also disappeared, and could not be found. But on the nineteenth day the mystery was explained, for walking in my orchard I happened to look between two tall hedges, and there, on a nest of dry leaves was the mother cat, with five beautiful kittens. Poor Ju had brought her here, had made the warm nest for her, and gone every day back to her old home and brought her a chicken. Ju had evidently reasoned that although Mrs. G— had turned her out, she ought to be well-fed at the expense of her mistress. Hence, the robbery of the chicken-roost.

mother. And when at last we were tired of romping, and
our beautiful mother went trotting back into the room
again, we were all glad enough to follow. What with the
exceeding brightness of the sun out of doors, we could not
see anything at all when we went inside. Night seemed to
have descended and enveloped us all in its darksome folds.
But mother, wiser than we, led us back to our cushion, and
no sooner did we lie down than we fell into a sound and
dreamless slumber.

So ended our first outing.

It became a regular thing now, however, this walk in
the garden, and seeing we enjoyed it so much, our mistress
and queen, whom the tall, black, red-eyed savage called
Beebee, took us out to revel among the sunshine and the
flowers every day; and every day brother and I seemed to
grow stronger and bigger.

I began to love Beebee very much too, and it was she
who named me Shireen.

Yes, Warlock, it is a strange name, and so would yours
appear to the people of Persia.

But one day, Beebee took me on her lap, and told me
why she had named me Shireen. " You must have a name,
my lovely flower," she said, in her sweet child voice, " so it
shall be Shireen. For know ye, that this was the name
held by the wife of a very great king and lord of Persia,
who lived ages and ages and ages ago, when this lovely
land was even greater than it is now."

I fear, my children, that I did not pay very much heed
to all Beebee was telling me, for I was very much taken up
with a string of pearls and rubies that she wore around her
beautiful arm just above the elbow, and all the time she
was speaking, I was chewing at it. But mother listened

and told me the tale of the Queen Shireen over again when
we were all by ourselves.

"I remember it," said a voice which wasn't Warlock's.
It was a voice that seemed to come from the clouds, and
a strange, sepulchral tone it had. "Yes, I remember it.
Just wait till I get down the chimney."

To say that every member of that circle of old friends
round the fire was startled would be a poor way of describing the general consternation.

A strange voice coming down the chimney! A weird,
sepulchral voice! And the owner of that voice was
going to follow it. He, she, or it, was coming down the
chimney!

Would the lights burn blue when the ghostly thing—the
dread apparition appeared?

"Eh? eh?" cried the starling. "What is it? What is
it? Tse, tse, tse!"*

Tabby's hair stood on end from tail to crown. Vee-Vee's
hair would have followed suit, only a Pomeranian's hair is
always on end, and fright even couldn't fix it a bit higher.
Shireen herself, being slightly imbued with superstition,
confessed afterwards that she felt a trifle uneasy as she
gazed at the chimney and waited.

The only really brave individual in the whole circle was
Warlock. There was nothing belonging to this world, or
even to a much worse world than ours, that could have
frightened Warlock. So he sprang up, faced the fire, and
barked.

"Don't be alarmed, any of you," said the voice in the
chimney. "It's only me. I'm coming down to tell you

---

* These were favourite expressions of my starling.

the story of Shireen, Queen of Persia. Bless you, I
remember her. It's only a matter of a thousand and a half
years——"

Here the creature was seized apparently with a fit of
coughing, and next moment he, she, or it, landed all in a
heap close to Shireen's footstool.

It was only Chammy after all, and everybody felt so
relieved.

" I daresay," he explained, "I've changed colour a bit.
Nothing unusual in a chameleon changing colour, is there,
Shireen, my furry dear?"

" No, Chammy, and you really have changed colour. Why,
you are as black as a sweep. Whatever made you creep
up the chimney?"

I may observe here, parenthetically, that Chammy was
sometimes found in the queerest places. You see, he had
the run of the room, and made strange use of it at times.

Once, for example, he disappeared for a whole week, and
was found at last hiding behind a large cobweb in Colonel
Clarkson's study. The Colonel was a humane sort of
man, you must know, and this particular cobweb belonged
to his pet spider, and was never touched. Oh, no, Chammy
had not eaten the spider; Chammy knew better than that.
The fact is, he had been studying that pet spider for weeks
perhaps, before he carried his scheme into execution.

I notice he must have said to himself, " That that big
spider never wants plenty of flies, and that she repairs her
web, after it has been broken by a blue-bottle fly, over-
night, and has it nice and new and fresh next morning fit

for another day's sport. Well, why should she have all the
blue-bottles? The blue-bottles are as much mine as hers.
Now, *I* can't build a web and catch them, but I can sit
snugly enough near hers, and when a blue-bottle comes I
can just touch him off. That sort of life will suit me far
better than catching my own flies, for I'm not so young as
I used to be a thousand years ago."

Another time Chammy had been away a whole month,
after partaking of about five-and-twenty meal-worms. The
Colonel felt sure he would never see his droll favourite
again; but one day he told the servant to put a little fire
in his study, and half an hour after that, Chammy was
found sitting on the fender, holding up his fingers and
palms to woo the welcome blaze.

In the sweet summer-time, Chammy was taken out of
doors and allowed to crawl on a grizzled old apple tree
that grew near to the study window. This used to please
Chammy very much, and he stalked flies with unerring
skill, and had plenty of exercise at the same time. The
strange point of the story is this: the tree was for the
most part grey and gnarled, so was Chammy, and a fly
would often alight right in front of him. Out would go
Chammy's tongue, slowly and steadily at first, then—pop!
and the fly would wonder where in all the world he had
got to. But there were large patches of green moss on the
apple tree, and Chammy dearly loved these because they
were warm and soft for his feet; but when resting on one,
he took the precaution to change colour to a beautiful sea-
green, and so the flies got licked in just the same. Well,
one evening, when Colonel Clarkson went to fetch Chammy
in, he couldn't find him high nor low; he looked on the
grey and gnarled parts of the tree, and he carefully

examined the patches of moss, and he even focussed his lorgnettes and scanned the tree up and down ; but no Chammy was to be seen, green or grey. So the Colonel put up his glasses with a sigh, saying to himself, "Some vagrant cat has no doubt taken my poor pet away."

Weeks flew by, and one evening while the kindly old soldier sat alone with his wife in the drawing-room, both very still, because they were reading and the children were away in the woods, lo! the cottage piano in the corner suddenly began to play.

Colonel Clarkson looked at his wife and his wife looked at the Colonel. Both, I think, were a little frightened, for when they glanced towards the piano there was nobody there.

But the ghostly music continued. It was strange, it was unaccountable and wonderful! The music was all on the descending scale, and chords were struck chiefly fifths. But the keys of the piano did not move, and the notes sounded far away. Presently the performance was concluded with a series of groans emitted by the bass strings.

"I have it," the Colonel cried, "it is Chammy. Dear old Chammy."

He jumped up and opened the instrument wide, and there sure enough was the chameleon. He had been asleep in there for three weeks or more, and had awakened hungry and lively—poor Chammy.

"Whatever made you get up the chimney, Chammy?" said Shireen again.

"Just to find a cosy corner," replied the chameleon, "for lor', bless your pretty face, Shireen, now that the days are getting shorter, my poor old toes do be that wondrous cold sometimes, you wouldn't believe."

"But you wanted to hear the story of Queen Shireen, didn't you?"

"Yes, Chammy, if you won't take long to tell it."

"Oh, not more'n a hundred years or so. Time is nothing to me, you know."

But time was a good deal to these old friends around the fire, so it ended after all in Chammy climbing up into his perch again, and apparently going to sleep there, with his droll eyes open, and Shireen herself having to tell the story.

CHAPTER V.

HOUGH Chammy talks about having been up in those days, said Shireen, when everybody was once more comfortably settled in his place, I don't really believe it, you know. For I think Chammy falls asleep and dreams things. Besides, Queen Shireen lived far longer ago than one thousand years. More nearly thirteen hundred years ago, my dear mistress Beebee told me.*

"You must know, dear Shireen," Beebee said as she smoothed my back and brow, "that in olden times Persia was a far grander country, and far more rich and warlike than it is now, and old King Chosroës I., the grandfather of Shireen's husband, reigned for fifty years in Persia, his wonderful palace being at Ctesiphon."

"Tse, tse, tse!" interrupted Dick.

Yes, Dick, said Shireen, I daresay you find that a hard word to remember. Well, the acts of Chosroës during the closing years of his long life are wonderful, for he not only expelled the Turkish hordes that had deigned

---

* Chosroës Parveez commenced his second reign Anno Domini 591.

to cross the Persian frontiers, but led an army against the greatest fortress that the Romans had in the south-east, and after tremendous fighting, that lasted for nearly six months, he captured it, and compelled the enemy to pay an indemnity of forty thousand pieces of gold.

I relate this story with conscious pride, my children, because, remember, I am a soldier's cat.

Well, Warlock, I daresay there were no Scotch terriers in those days,* for while Persia was in the height of its glory, Britain was inhabited by a race, or rather many races, who knew very little indeed of civilization. Don't be angry, Warlock. Well, children, the old king was succeeded by his son, Hormazd, who celebrated his coronation by putting all his brothers to death. This was certainly not very humane, but it was the common practice in those days, and it probably saved the reigning king's life, for poisoned cups and daggers were much used in olden times as an easy way of securing accession to estates and thrones.

Nevertheless this new king was tolerant of Christianity, and this itself speaks in his favour. However, he committed one mistake, and this cost him his throne ; for one of his greatest generals happening to lose a battle, as any general might once in a way, he degraded him by sending him the dress and the distaff of an old woman. " Wear these, general," was the message that accompanied the gift. " Give up war now and take to spinning."

---

* The author begs to say that he believes Shireen may be wrong about the Scotch terriers. For in a hotel in Surrey there is a beautiful engraving of a picture by one of the old masters—he can't say which old master—called "Noah alighting from the Ark." Well, Noah is surrounded by his family, and accompanied by two Scotch collie dogs, good enough to win a prize anywhere. Question : If there were Scotch collies, why not Scotch terriers?

Now this general was the hero of a hundred fights, so he now swore revenge, and marched with an army against the king's capital. This was the beginning of the end of Hormazd's reign. The end itself soon came, and a terrible one it was. The army that Hormazd sent against the general mutinied. Then the maternal uncle of Chosroës, the son of the king, arose and threw Hormazd into prison. A prison in those days was a vile and slimy dark dungeon, alive with vermin of every description. It was soon darker still for poor Hormazd, because men came at night and blinded him with red-hot wires. Death was surely a relief to him after this. And it soon came. He was murdered, and his son reigned in his stead.

It has been said that Chosroës II. had had some hand in his father's death, but Beebee, my mistress, did not believe this, neither must we. We should be charitable. Besides, I don't think that if Chosroës had given orders for his father's execution, that he would have condemned his uncle to death as soon as he mounted the throne.

But Chosroës II. became a very great king, or shah, though in the end, very unfortunate.

For my own part, continued Shireen after a little pause, I would rather have been a cat than a king in those days. It does seem very sad that although Chosroës II. was a great conqueror, and expelled the fighting power of Rome from both Asia and Africa, that although he elevated his own country to perhaps the highest rank it had ever held, he should have lived to see Persia ruined. He himself was thrown into prison. Oh! the pity of it, children; and his favourite sons and daughters brought in and murdered before his face.

Shireen, his queen, was the one only wife he had ever loved.

And what a fearful fall was his! Remember that he was a very great king, a very mighty conqueror, and his whole story reads like one of the grandest of old romances. It is too long for a poor pussy cat like me to tell, but I heard my master only yesterday say to Lizzie and Tom, that they must read histories like that of Persia in the days of its glory, if they would really enjoy chivalry and romance combined, and Lizzie says she is sure she will, and Tom too, when they get a little older.

But Chosroës was at the height of his glory after he had cowed and conquered the proud Romans, depriving them of every foot of territory won by their legions under Cæsar and Pompey and many others.

And nothing could exceed the splendour of his court and palace at Ctesiphon, nor the extent of his wealth and riches.

The Persians do not turn night into day. They live naturally, go to bed early and get up while the morning is still in its pristine beauty; and this healthful practice was in fashion even in the days of Chosroës II. And it was at sunrise, in his splendid pavilion, that this king and conqueror gave audience. From Arabia, from Egypt, from Mesopotamia, from Armenia, yea, from east and west, and north and south, flocked couriers to these audiences. And there the king would be to receive them, and at his side the beautiful and virtuous Shireen; while around him were gathered in robes of state his generals, his wise men, and his nobles of every rank, all proud of their great lord and master, yet trembling at every word he uttered; while each minute there sped from the gates of the magnificent palace swift horsemen, bearing to every nook of his vast dominions the commands of this mighty king.

But the luxury of this palace, the art displayed, the carvings, mosaics, the draperies, the ornamentation of every summer or winter room or saloon, and the voluptuous splendour and comfort, what tongue could describe?

Some notion of the extent of the palace and its magical surroundings may be gathered from the fact that three thousand ladies-in-waiting lived in or around the vast and luxurious fort, and that these had twelve thousand hand-maidens to wait upon them. But the stables must have been a marvellous show. Fancy, Warlock, twelve thousand white camels, a thousand lordly elephants, and fifty thousand horses, asses, and mules.

"Tse, tse, tse!" from Dick once more.

"You well may marvel, Dick darling."

But alas! and alas! the tide took a turn, and all the glory of Chosroës ended in gloomy tragedy.

The fortunes of Rome were at the lowest ebb in 617 A.D. The warriors of Persia were actually within a mile—of water—of the capital, and Herodius, the emperor, had already sent away his family and his treasures, and was himself preparing to fly, when, instigated by his people and their patriarch, he took a solemn oath to do or die for Rome.

> " And when can men die better,
> Than in facing fearful odds,
> For the ashes of their fathers,
> And the country of their Gods:"

The Persians were getting ready their fleet to cross that silvery streak. The Romans had a fleet. That fleet was the beginning of the salvation of Rome and the overthrow of mighty Chosroës. Herodius sailed on Easter Monday

622 A.D. for the Gulf of Issus, with the remains of his shattered army, and the great general and hero, Shahr Barz, made haste to annihilate the Romans and their emperor. But these fought with all the energy and fury of despair, and—the Persians were beaten.

Down, down, down went Chosroës now. His own people at last revolted against him, and he was thrown into a vile dungeon called the Dungeon of Darkness. Bread and water was his only fare, and even the officers of his guard spat upon and reviled him. He was led forth at last, suffered every indignity, and was tortured to death.

His only consolation in his terrible imprisonment in that dark and loathsome dungeon, was the thought that his beautiful Queen Shireen was dead.

Nay, she was not dead, she had gone before. For Shireen was not only a beautiful and good woman, but a Christian in every sense of the word.

But although so many hundreds of years have fled since then, far away in the palatial homes of Persia, and in the humbler houses of her sons and daughters, bards and minstrels sing to this day of the deeds of the hero-king, bold Chosroës, and of the love he bore for sweet Shireen.

CHAPTER VI.

"NA, LASS," SAID CRACKER, "I'LL NO DRINK THE LITTLE 'UN'S MILK."

UT it is time, said Shireen, that I should return to the home of my dear mistress, the beautiful young Beebee, and the events of my own early days. It may be thought a descent from the heroic, and yet I don't know, Warlock; for you know a cat, or even a Scotch terrier, may show real heroism at times.

I do not want to boast, but I must tell you, children, that I once had a terrible encounter with a wild lion in the forest, and that I came off victorious. Oh, dear me, I should not have nerve enough for so awful an adventure now, but then I knew not what fear was.

My lovely mistress then used to take me out into the woods with her. She rode upon a charming milk-white steed, with tail and mane dyed crimson, and was attended by many armed horsemen. I used to sit in front of her on the saddle.

But one day a bird on a bough that bent very low over us attracted my attention, while Shireen stopped her horse, and was talking to one of her armed attendants.

I sprang at once into the tree to seize the bird, that I might take it home in triumph to my mother. Alas! I not only missed my bird, but I lost my mistress.

For when I descended the bough again no one was there. The whole cavalcade had ridden on. What should I do? I ran hither and thither, mewing and crying in terror and anguish, but no one came near me. Had I been an older cat I might easily have found my way back. But I was then only four months old, and knew not what to do, or which way to turn.

I descended to the ground, however, and did the best thing perhaps that I could have done. I sat down on the greensward and determined to wait. My mistress, I felt sure, would send back for me as soon as she missed me.

But, as ill-luck would have it, a small nut fell from a tree close to my nose. I jumped to my feet in a moment. What a game I did have to be sure with that nut! My mistress, my mother, every creature in the world was forgotten in the mad excitement of that merry game. I played and played till the shades of evening fell around me, then tired, exhausted, and hungry, yet not knowing where to look for food, I threw myself down under a bush and went fast asleep.

I awoke at last, though how long I had slept I could not tell, nor could I tell my whereabouts, for in my mad merry game I must have gone miles away from the spot where I had been lost. I was lost now, indeed! And I was also dreadfully frightened, for the forest all around me resounded with the cries and the roaring of wild beasts. I had heard my mother speak of these, and how terrible they all were, and how quickly they could cranch the life out of the biggest cat that ever lived. But, strange to say, I was not a bit afraid.

The moon was shining as bright as day, so I got up and determined I would try to find my way out of the awful forest. Luck favoured me for once. Not that my situation was changed much for the better, for I now found myself in a broad or treeless waste ; but the awful noise of the wild beasts no longer confused me, and I thought I would soon be home.

That plain was wider far than I had any idea of, and when the moon went down at last, after walking some distance further, I once more lay down to sleep. It was grey dawn when I awoke, and found I was not far from another forest. This I entered. But I had not gone far when a loud peal of thunder seemed to shake the earth to its very foundation, and I thought for a moment that the trees were going to fall upon me and crush my life out. I looked up, and lo ! instead of thunder I found that the awful sound proceeded from a monster cat with eyes like yellow fire, and great teeth as thick as my tail.

I knew it was a lion, so I determined to slay him where he stood, and advanced towards him with this bold intent.

I arched my back to make myself look as terrible as possible, and my hair standing all on end made me look double the size. Then I growled, but not *quite* so loud as the lion. The lion had lain down for a spring, but I am sure he had never seen the like of me before.

On I marched, half sideways.

The lion looked droll and puzzled.

I was within a yard of him now, still walking half sideways, with arched back and one foot in the air. I did this for effect.

"Fuss-ss ! Fut ! Sphut !"

I jumped directly at his face. But I never got near

WITH A YELL OF TERROR HE SPRANG HIGH IN THE AIR.

him. With a yell of terror he sprang high in the air, then made off into the dark depths of the forest as fast as his four legs could carry him.

My adventure was over, for I saw him no more; but oh, joy! half-an-hour after this, just as the beautiful sun was rising, red and rosy, over the wooded hills, something as white as snow came feathering along towards me. It was my own dear blue-eyed mother, and in two hours' time I was safely home again and on my little mistress's lap.

'The days and weeks flew by, oh, so quickly at my Persian home, and when I look back to them now it is with some degree of regret that I did not then realise my happiness. It is ever thus, and even mankind himself laments the loss of his youth. The days of the young are golden, their pathway leads over the soft sward; there are flowers at every side and trees nod green above; beyond is the azure sky, and the young think that storms will never arise, that their path will aye be smooth, that the trees will never be stripped of their foliage, nor the bright flowers cease to blow. Alas! and alas! for the dreams of youth.

Well, my youth or my kittenhood came to an end. And I think it came all at once. I was in the garden one day all by myself, when suddenly I was confronted with a monster brown rat of a breed that grows larger in Persia, they tell me, than anywhere else in the world.

Will you believe me, children, when I tell you that I felt more afraid of that rat than I had been of the lion? The awful beast did not even run away, and I knew it would be a battle to the bitter end.

"Only you, is it?" he said. "Fiss! I'm not afraid of a kitten. Your father killed my brother, and I mean to be revenged on you. Fiss!"

Then the fight began. How long it lasted I do not know. But in the end I was conqueror. What mattered it that I was bitten all about the face and feet, or my beautiful white coat bedabbled with blood!

Oh, that was a proud moment when I rushed in to my mother's presence dragging my dead enemy across the mosaic floor. He was far too big to lift and carry.

I came in growling, feeling every inch a heroine. Nor would I permit my brother to touch my rat. My mother seemed very proud of me now, and as soon as the slave came and carried away the trophy of my triumph, mother commenced to clean my coat and bathe my wounds with her soft warm tongue. I was soon well, but felt another being now, and would have been quite ashamed to play any longer with my mother. I even deserted the cushion on which I had slept so long, and slept higher up on an ottoman.

I now attached myself more and more to my young mistress Beebee, and I became her favourite and her pet. I was almost constantly by her side during the day, except when on the warpath slaying huge rats, and I always occupied her lovely sleeping apartment at night.

But young though she was, Beebee was never idle. And her story which she told me one day, weeping bitterly, was, I thought, a very sad one.

"My own Shireen," she said, "you see how hard at work they keep me. For to me, Shireen, study is indeed the hardest of work. But my teachers seldom leave me. I have a European lady to teach me English. This is the

best of it, and oh, how I wish I were English, and free ; as
it is, I am but a slave. But this dear lady is good to me,
and gives me lovely fairy-tale books to read in her own
language ; but yet these I must hide from the fierce-eyed
eunuchs who guard me night and day. I am also taught
music, the piano, and the zither, and I am taught to sing.
Then a scion of the prophet—that old, old man with the
long dyed beard, and the cloak of camel's hair—teaches
me Sanscrit and the higher branches of the Persian, so that
my poor little head is turned, and my night is often passed
in weeping and dreaming.

"I have no mother, my sweet Shireen. Look at these
pearls and rubies and amethysts ; I would give them all,
all to have a mother, if only for a month."

I purred and sung to Beebee, but she would not be
comforted.

"I tell my story to you, Shireen, though you are only a
cat. But I must speak to some one who loves me, else I
soon would die."

Here her tears fell faster and faster.

"And oh, Shireen, I have not told you the worst.

"It is this, Shireen. Those beautiful English books tell
me that in England a man has someone to love and care
for him, someone whose lot in life is the same as his ;
that someone is his life. But here in Persia—oh! Shireen,
Shireen—if one is as I am, the daughter of a noble, and if
she is beautiful and clever, her lot is indeed a hard one.
She is sold—yes, sold is the right name, to the Shah.

"My father is cold-hearted and cruel. I seldom see
him. He is ever, ever at Court, and when in the hunting
season he brings a party to this lovely castle I am hidden
away. And why, think you, Shireen? It is because when

I grow older and cleverer in a few years' time I shall go in state to the Shah. My prince will never come, as he always does, in beautiful English books; he will never come to bear me away. I shall be but one of a thousand, and spend a life like a bulbul in a golden cage.

" I have no one that loves me but you, Shireen. And now, lest they take you from me, I am going to mark you. Oh, my beautiful cat, it will not hurt. The magician himself will insert a tiny ruby in one of your teeth, Shireen ; then if they take you away because I love you so, and bring me another cat like you, I can say, ' No, no, this is not Shireen ; give me back Shireen.' And no peace will they have until you are restored."

Well, children, the magician took me from Beebee, and he put me into a deep trance, and in one of my teeth he drilled a hole and inserted a tiny ruby.

That ruby is there now, and ever will remain.

"Just look at that happy group, Mrs. Clarkson," said Uncle Ben, "and that wonderful cat in the midst of them. Wouldn't you think she had been, or *is* talking to them ? "

" Well," said Mrs. Clarkson, " I shouldn't really wonder if animals that are so much together day after day as these are, have a sort of language of their own."

" A kind of animal Volapuk," said the Colonel laughing. " Well, it may be, you know, but I am of opinion, and have long been so, that animals have souls. Oh, surely God never meant affection and love such as theirs, and truth and faithfulness to rot in the ground."

" Well, I can't say, you know," said Uncle Ben.

"There is my cockatoo here."

"Oh, pardon me for interrupting you, my sailor friend, but a cockatoo hasn't half the sense and sagacity a cat has."

"Poor Cockie wants to go to bed!"—This from the bird on Ben's shoulder.

"Hear that?" cried Ben laughing.

"When you can make your cat give utterances to such a sensible remark as that, I'll—but, my dear soldier, it is eleven o'clock, and Tom and Lizzie, poor little dears, have both dropped off to sleep. Good night!"

"Good night! Good night!" shrieked the cockatoo in a voice that waked the children at once. "Good night. Cockie's off. Cockie's off."

And away went the sailor.

But next morning Shireen had an adventure that very nearly put a stop to her story-telling for ever.

She had gone off after breakfast for a ramble in the green fields and through the village. It happened to be Saturday, so there was no school to-day, and just as she was coming out of the cottage where the sick child was, and promising herself a nap in Uncle Ben's hammock, who should she see coming up the street with her little brother in a tall perambulator, but her favourite schoolgirl, Emily Stoddart.

Up marched Shireen with her tail in the air.

"Oh, you dear lovely pussy!" cried Emily, lifting her up and placing her in the perambulator, when she at once commenced to sing, greatly to the delight of the child.

And away went Emily wheeling them both.

"Oh, dear, what shall we do, Shireen?" cried Emily next moment, trying to hide pussy with a shawl. "Here comes the butcher's awful dog."

The bull-terrier made straight for the perambulator.

"Come down out o' there at once," he seemed to cry.
" I've got you now.   You'll be a dead 'un in half-a-minute
more."

"You won't?   Then here goes."

The bull-terrier—and he was no small weight either—
made a spring for the perambulator.   Emily made a spring
to save the child.   Danger had no intention, however, of
harming a hair in that child's head.   It was the cat Shireen
he was after ; the cat, the cat, and no one else.

The child swayed to one side to save himself, and next
moment down went his carriage.   Down went cat and
carriage, the child and Emily, and the bull-terrier, all
mixed up in one confused heap.

Shireen was the first to extricate herself and to bolt for
her life, but Danger was the next, and it did not seem that
poor pussy's span of existence was at that moment worth
an hour's purchase.

For a cat to permit herself to be caught by a dog while
running away is the worst possible policy for the cat,
because the pursuer gets her by the back and the spine
is broken.   Shireen knew this, and she also knew there
was no way of escape handy, no railing to run through, no
doorway to enter, no tree to climb, so she determined to
sell her life dearly.

Round she turned, and the blow she caught that dog
staggered him for a little, and the blood ran over his face.

All in vain though.   He came on now with redoubled
ferocity, and down went poor Shireen.

Emily screamed and flew to her assistance.

But in two seconds more a true hero came to the rescue.
This was none other save Cracker himself, the large Airdale
terrier.

" Here, lad ! " cried Cracker, or seemed to cry in good
broad honest Yorkshire English. " What's tha' doin' wi'
t'ould cat ? "

He did not give the butcher's dog time to reply, but,
seizing him by the back of the neck, shook him as if he
had been a rat.

Never in his life before had Danger received so severe a
chastisement. In three minutes' time he was running down
the street on three legs, and all covered with blood and
dust.

Shireen quietly reseated herself in the baby's carriage,
and Emily didn't know what to do with perfect joy. She
got Cracker round the neck and positively hugged him.

" Oh, you dear good noble dog," she cried. " Here, you
must have a drop of milk."

She took the child's bottle, poured a little into her hand,
and held it out to Cracker.

But Cracker only shook his head.

" Na, lass, na," he said. " I'll come and see thee now
and then, but— I'll no drink the little 'un's milk."

A rougher-looking and more unkempt tyke than Cracker
you might have wandered a long way without meeting. Yet
he hid under that towsy exterior of his a kind and generous
heart. And from that day Emily, he, and Shireen were
the best of friends.

Cracker would meet the girl in the street and walk up,
laughing all over apparently, and shaking his thick stob of
a docked tail till it seemed to retaliate and shake the dog.

" How's things this mornin', Emily ? " he seemed to say.
" And how's the little 'un ? You haven't got t'ould cat
to-day then. Well, good-bye. I'm just off."

And away he would trot.   E

CHAPTER VII.

BEBEE'S FATE IS SEALED.

T was a day or two after, that Shireen once more met her friends, but this time it was on the sunny lawn in front of Uncle Ben's bungalow.

They were all there except Chammy the chameleon. No one knew for the present where he was. He had eaten an extra supply of meal-worms and flies the day before, and forthwith disappeared. In a fortnight's time perhaps, he might be found in the fold of a curtain, or behind the ventilator in the Colonel's study, or he might be brought up from the cellar in a scuttle of coals, or tumble out of a bag of flour when the cook went to make a dumpling, for no one could ever say for certain where Chammy might or might not be.

But on this particular afternoon Colonel Clarkson and Uncle Ben were drinking iced sherbert, and smoking their pipes in peace at a little wicker table under the shadow of the great chestnut tree.

Warlock and Tabby had just come back from a long ramble in the woods, and thrown themselves down beside Shireen and her foster son, Vee-Vee, the Pomeranian.

Cockie, and Dick, the starling, were bandying words together on the gowany lawn.*

It would have been very difficult indeed for a stranger to have told whether they were quarrelling or not.

One thing is certain, they were each of them trotting out all the words in their somewhat limited vocabulary for the other's benefit, no matter whether they were relevant or not.

Dick was much more active than Cockie, and ran round and round him on the lawn, pausing occasionally to thrust his beak into the ground, and opening it out like a pair of compasses, peep into the hole to see if a worm were at home.

I have said that Dick kept running round and round Cockie. He certainly described a circle about two yards from the cockatoo—he knew better than to come any nearer, for the big bird had a punishing beak—but seeing that Cockie in the centre went wheeling about, and always faced Dick, it becomes a question whether Dick actually did go round him. What do you think?

And all the while the two kept talking.

Not that their conversation was very edifying. I shall give you a sample.

Dick.—(After swallowing a worm six inches long.) " Tse, tse, tse, tse ! Pretty Dick ! Pr—r—r—etty Dick !

Cockie.—" Pretty Cockie !"

Dick.—" Dick's a darling starling, master's pretty pet."

Cockie.—" Poo—oor Cockie !"

Dick.—" Eh ? Eh ? What is it ? What d'ye say ? Tse, tse, tse ! You rr—r—rascal ! "

* The gowan is the mountain daisy.

Cockie.—" Cockie wants to go to bed !"

Dick.—" You r—rascal ! Sugar, snails, and sop ! What is it, you r—rascal ? Whew, whew, whew " (whistling).

Cockie (singing).—" Lal de lal, de dal, de dal."

Dick (talking very fast).—" Dick's a darling ! Dick's a starling ! Dick's a master's pretty pet, sugar, snails, and pretty sop ; you r—r—rascal !"

Dick now hauls out an extra long worm.

Cockie shrieks as if he had seen a snake. Dick, frightened out of his wits, lets go the worm, and flies off to perch on the tabby cat's glossy back, and commences—a favourite trick of his—to go through the motions of having a bath.

" Well, Mother Shireen," says Warlock.

" Well, children, so you've got back ?"

" Oh, Mother Shireen, what a day we've been having !" says Tabby.

" Yes," cries Warlock, " it's been an out and outer."

" You haven't been naughty, I hope ?"

" Oh, no, that is not particularly. But I chased Mother Maver's old grey cat, though I didn't mean to have done so ; but what does she always want to spit at me for I want to know ? And I jumped at Farmer Dobbs' game cock, and nearly had him by the tail. Oh, didn't he skraigh just ! and didn't the chickens fly ! And then old Farmer Dobbs flew at me with the garden rake. But I don't care, for his cock once struck me on the head with his foot and made a hole in it. Then Tab and I went to the woods. It is fine fun being in the woods. We found a wild bees' hive. Honey is so nice, though Tab doesn't care for it. But I soon had the combs out, and I'm afraid I killed all the bees. Twenty settled on my back, then I rolled over and over with my heels in the air, and that settled them.

We went to the weasel's nest, but the weasel must have seen us coming. Weasels are wily, you know. But Tab killed a wild pigeon, and I killed a mole. We tried to get a rabbit, but couldn't. Then we spent a whole hour trying to catch a water rat, but they are wily like the weasels, and the door of their house is deep down under the water. Tab isn't much good in the water, but you can't beat her in a tree. Some day we are going to ask Cracker to come with us to the water-rat's bank, and we'll sink a mine, and then see if the rats can make fools of Tab and me. On our way back, we passed old Farmer Dobbs' place again, and then we had it out."

" Had what out ? " said Vee-Vee.

" Why the game-cock's tail. He was in a field with his hens, and said something cheeky to us as we passed, and I went for him. He flew up into a tree, but Tab soon had him down out of that. Tab is simply a treat in a tree. Then I grabbed him by the tail, and, oh, didn't the feather fly just ! You *would* have laughed. We left in rather a hurry, because old Farmer Dobbs went in to get his gun. We shan't go Farmer Dobbs' way again for a whole fortnight. But come, Shireen, tell us a little more of your story. You left yourself at Beebee's beautiful palace in Persia."

Yes, said Shireen, and soon after that ruby had been placed in my tooth, an event occurred that altered the whole course of my life, and of poor Beebee's too.

I do not know how old Beebee was at this time, but I think she must have been about twelve, and she appeared to me to get more and more beautiful every day.

Now, never during all my lifetime had I seen Beebee's father, and I was now over six months old ; but one day

great preparations were being made at the palace, slaves
and servants were running about everywhere, and the lovely
saloons were decorated with flowers, and hung round with
many coloured lamps. I was not therefore surprised to be
told by Beebee that her father was about to pay a visit to
his home, previous to accompanying the Shah on a long
journey to Europe, and over to England itself.

"Oh, how much I should like to go," she sighed, "and
if I did, you too, my sweet Shireen, should accompany
me."

Then one forenoon the father arrived in great state, with
many camels and horses, and even accompanied by several
elephants. With him came many other great men and
dignitaries of the court, and they feasted for many days
together. But all this time my poor little mistress was
confined to her apartments.

One day—this was his only visit—Beebee's father came
to see her.

He was indeed a noble-looking man, and splendidly
dressed in silken robes of many colours, and a cloak of
camel's hair, from under which peeped out a richly-
jewelled sword-hilt. On his head was a gilded turban ;
on his feet were beautiful sandals.

Beebee ran to meet him, and stood before him with
downcast eyes. She was prepared to rush into his arms
and be embraced, but he only smiled and coldly took her
hand.

Then he sank into an ottoman with graceful ease, whilst
she remained standing by his side.

"My daughter grows taller, and she grows beautiful.
She has a happy future before her. I have come to say
farewell for a time. I have a long journey, and many

long voyages before me. Beebee will see me when I return."

Then she dropped on her knees before him, and clasping her hands as if in prayer, held them up towards him.

" My father," she began.

He was frowning.

" My father is the most noble and handsome man in all the world. His sword is the sharpest sword in Persia. The arm that wields it is the strongest in all the wide dominions of the mighty Shah. If my father had enemies they would flee before him. But this is impossible, for all who see my father love him, and the Shah himself delights to bask in the sunshine of his smile."

" My daughter speaks truly," he said, relenting a little, " she speaks the white, pure truth ; but what would she of me ? "

" Oh, my father, you have but one little daughter, and she wants to love you dearly. She would be more in your presence. Beebee wants to see the world. Take her with you to Europe, to England. She would fain see England. She——"

" Bah ! " he interrupted. " Who hath put such foolish notions in your head ? Have you not an English teacher? She can tell you all you desire to know. My daughter knows not what she asks."

" Oh, my father ! "

" Silence, child ! Silence ! You are intended for the court of the Shah. The touch of unbelieving fingers, nay, even the glance of a foreigner's eye would defile my daughter's caste. No longer then would she be fit to stand before the king of kings, our great lord and master, the Shah."

" Father, father, I will not be bride to the Shah !"

" What! This to me ? "

He sprang up as he spoke, and I trembled lest he should strike my little mistress to the earth. He towered above her, as the poplar tree towers above the linden.

But he only strode to the arched and curtained doorway. He turned round as he went out, holding the drapery in his left hand.

" Adieu !" he said. " Adieu ! My daughter must obey me, or——"

" Or what, father ? "

Once more her hands were extended pleadingly, prayerfully towards him.

" She *dies !* "

The drapery fell. Beebee's father had gone, and she had thrown herself on the ottoman cushions to weep.

I walked softly towards her, I sung to her ; I licked her little white fingers. Then she ceased to weep.

" Oh, Shireen! Shireen !" she cried, "this is a bitter, bitter day to me. And I wanted to love father so. I could love him so. I have no mother. I——"

She threw herself down once more, and sobbed aloud.

I felt that I could have suffered anything to comfort and solace my beautiful mistress.

But what could I do?

I was only a cat.

Poor Beebee, she fell asleep there at last, and the red sunset clouds were in the sky before she awoke once more.

CHAPTER VIII.

LIFE IN A TURRET HIGH.—STRANGE ADVENTURE IN THE FOREST.

BEEBEE'S father was gone, and peace and quiet reigned once more in the palace.

But the poor child fell ill.

Now the house or palace where Beebee lived was a somewhat lonesome one, and many, many miles from the town, though not a great way from the village. It stood on elevated ground, surrounded by splendid gardens, in which grew the rarest of tropical fruits and flowers. Away behind it was the everlasting forest, and behind that the snow-capped mountains, raising their jagged summits into the blue ethereal sky.

But from the turrets high, away to the west, glimpses of the sea could be had, and almost every evening Beebee and I went up to see the sunset. It was glorious, Beebee said, to look upon the ocean at any time, but to behold it lit up with the reflections of the gold and the crimson clouds, was like having a glimpse of Paradise.

A physician was now sent for from the distant town, and his words to Beebee were words of wisdom.

"It is not medicine I will give my fair young patient,"

he said. "It is not medicine that she needs. It is the soul that is sick, not the body. But if the body is strengthened the soul will become calm. My patient grieves for an absent father, perhaps."

Beebee sighed, and the tears stole into her eyes.

"She must seek for surcease of sorrow every day in the forest," continued the physician. "Let her go with armed attendants, for wild beasts are many, deep in the dark woodland recesses."

Then Beebee smiled through her tears.

"In the turret high," she said, "one can catch glimpses of the ever-changing sea."

"Yes, yes, my patient may go there often."

"I would sleep there."

"Good. My patient shall. So now adieu! I will come again."

"You are wise and good," said Beebee innocently. "I shall pray for you."

"Ah! then," he replied, "all good fortune will attend me. If one so young and guileless prays for poor me, the gods will not forget me. Adieu!"

"Adieu!"

Miss Morgan entered softly when the physician went away. She was Beebee's English teacher. Beebee flew to meet her, and told her all the doctor had said.

"It is what he likewise told me," said Miss Morgan, "and your studies are to be interrupted for a time. Your teacher of Sanscrit shall come no more for months. You will have a long holiday, and I am to read you books that will amuse instead of instructing you."

"And I am to have a chamber in the turret?"

"Yes, dear, it is already being draped."

"Oh! now indeed I begin to feel well and happy."

And in the exuberance of her joy Beebee hung around Miss Morgan's neck and danced up and down like a little child.

It was very pleasant up there in that turret, high above the swaying trees.

Although so high above everything the room was by no means a small one. Like those below, too, it was beautifully draped and tapestried, and the floor was of mosaics, crimson and blue and yellow, while the cushions that surrounded the walls were soft and delightful.

And all around the broad balcony the autumn roses clustered and clung, while the sweet odour of orange blossoms was wafted up from the gardens below. It was like new life to Beebee to dwell up in this turret high. There was so much to be seen that would never have been visible in the lower rooms.

The trees in themselves were a study, and that too, a very beautiful one. Probably no country in the world has more lovely woods than those of Persia. Here they were in all shapes; some on cliff tops, looking like noble pillared temples encanopied with dark masses of foliage; some like waves of the great rolling ocean itself; some like clouds of living green; while trees near at hand were seen to be hung and festooned with wild flowers, rich and rare, with which the sward itself was patched, and painted, and parterred. And every flower seemed to have a specially coloured moth or butterfly, or swift-winged dragon fly, that flew or floated or darted in the sunshine above it. And every bush seemed to contain a bird, the music of their voices as they answered each other in love songs, being, Beebee told me, ravishing to the ear, though I fear that I,

being but a cat, and a young one, did not sufficiently
appreciate the melody, and viewed the songsters themselves more from an epicurean and edible point of view
than any other. Some of the birds were most lovely, and
brighter in wing than the rainbow, that in more gloomy
weather hung over the distant woodlands.

Strange as it may seem to you, Tabby, and to you, Mr.
Warlock, the birds around my Persian home were very
tame indeed. The reason for this is not far to seek.
They were neither hunted nor worried, and even the
peasantry, in the mud villages, looked upon them as sacred,
and their songs as God-gifts.

> "God's poets, hid in foliage green,
>   Singing endless songs, themselves unseen;
> May we not dream God sends them there,
>   Mellow angels of the air?"

No, they were not hunted and killed, nor were their
nests robbed and rent in pieces by village rustics, and so
they were tame, and seemed to love the people among
whom they dwelt.

All night long the bulbuls sang, and at daybreak
Beebee and I were awakened from our slumbers by the
murmuring music of little bronze-winged pigeons that sat
on our turret balcony. And at any hour of the day if
Beebee went out upon the balcony and waved a dainty
handkerchief towards the woods, birds of all kinds came
flocking around her, sat on the balcony rail, alighted on
her head, on her shapely white arms, and even fed from
her open palm.

Yes, I confess that my instinct did at times whisper to
me that I should seize upon one of these lovely birds and

bear it away into some quiet corner and munch it and eat it, feathers and all.

But the very heinousness of such a crime used to make me shudder and draw further back into the turret chamber. Kill Beebee's birds! How terrible! As dreadful as if Tabby yonder were to slay poor droll Dick, of whom we are each and all so fond.

But even birds of prey used to hover high above the turret at times, and wait until Beebee threw pieces of bread towards them. Then down they would swoop as swift as arrows, and the tit-bits had not time to reach the ground before they were seized and borne away to the woods.

The woods, and the birds, and the wild flowers, these alone would have rendered our turret life an ideal one. But there was the sky also, a never-ending, ever-changing source of delight to Beebee.

We were up here in the clouds almost, for so high was the turret that often we could see little fleecy cloudlets resting over the trees in the valley far beneath. The sunrises in the east, where mountain rose o'er mountain, and hills on hills, till they hid their snowy heads in the heavens, were indescribably grand and gorgeous. Long, long before the sun itself uprose, and while the shadows of night still rested in valleys and glens, those snow-covered peaks, all jagged and toothed, were lighted up with the most delicate shades of pink and crimson, with ethereal shadows of pearly blue. Downwards and downwards the light and colour would creep, till the forests seemed to swim in a purple haze; then bars and fleeces of cloud grew before our eyes from grey to bronze, and from bronze to lake and gold, and presently the sun's red disc shimmered over the horizon and it was day; and the whole woods awakened at once into a burst of joyous bird-music and melody.

The sunsets used to be equally lovely.

Beebee would watch the sea all day long almost. It never was lacking in charm for her, whether grey under clouds of pearl, or bright blue under a cloudless sky, or dark with trailing thunderstorms, it was always the sea; and when a ship appeared, she would clap her tiny hands for very joy, and run to procure her lorgnettes, that she might even see the sailors as they walked to and fro across the decks, or leant listlessly over the bulwarks.

"Some day, some day," she would cry, "some day, dear Shireen, you and I will be on the ocean, and then, oh! then, at last, I shall be free. I have been by its banks, Shireen, and have heard the music of its waters. But it has a secret, a secret that it tells only to those who brave its dangers.

> "'Wouldst thou, the helmsman answered,
>   Learn the secrets of the sea?
>   Only those who brave its dangers,
>   Comprehend its mystery.'

"But," she added, still quoting the American bard :—

> "'Ah ! what pleasant visions haunt me
>   As I gaze upon the sea !
>   All the old romantic legends,
>   All my dreams come back to me.
>
> 'Sails of silk and ropes of sendal,
>   Such as gleam in ancient lore ;
>   And the singing of the sailors,
>   And the answers from the shore.

" ' Till my soul is filled with longing
        For the secret of the sea ;
    And the heart of that great ocean
        Sends a thrilling pulse through me.' "

Yet beautiful though the sunsets used to be they seemed ever to throw a shadow of melancholy over Beebee's heart, and whether Miss Morgan was in the room or not, she would sit at the balcony casement in dreamy silence long after the glory of the clouds had left them, and the shades of night were falling over sea and land.

Then the stars would glimmer out, and their light appeared always to make her happy once more. The evening star was her especial favourite, not because it is the star of love, but because she called it and thought it her mother's eye.

She would make her governess repeat to her, often over and over again, Longfellow's beautiful lines to this star :—

"Just above yon sandy bar,
    As the day grows fainter and dimmer,
Lonely and lovely a single star
    Lights the air with a dusky glimmer.

"Into the ocean faint and far,
    Falls the trail of its golden splendour ;
And the gleam of that single star,
    Is ever refulgent, soft, and tender."

Yes, I think Beebee loved that star better even than she loved the moon that in silver radiance used to shine softly, dreamily down on the woods and wilds.

My children, continued Shireen after a pause, I dwell longer on these pleasant scenes than perhaps I ought to ;

for, ah! me, this was the happiest part of my existence, and now that I am old and know I must soon sleep beneath the daisies, the thought of my ideal life then cheers my heart and banishes sadness far away.

But a change came. You must know then, Warlock, that Beebee did not neglect the advice the good physician had given her, and that every day she rode out into the woods and into the forests, always with a retinue of armed servants.

Why such a retinue, did you ask, Warlock? Well, I think there were two reasons. One was that the eunuch, who was Beebee's special guardian, had received from her father strict injunctions never to let her beyond his ken ; another was that the country some distance from the palace was infested by roving banditti, and that these robbers were sometimes in the pay of dissolute nobles, and would think but little of attacking a cavalcade, if they thought themselves strong enough to overpower it, and bearing away with them a young lady as prisoner.

But Beebee had not the slightest fear for herself. Her father was bold and brave to a fault. The daughter was brave without being bold. She bore but little good-will now, however, to that fierce-eyed black guardian of hers, and when out in the forest she was mischievous enough to give him many a fright. Beebee, you must know, was a great favourite with all her father's retainers, and she used to bribe the chief groom sometimes to saddle for her a very fleet horse, and to let Jazr the black eunuch have but a sorry one. Then she would touch her horse with her spurs of gold when far away in the forest, and laughingly calling to Jazr to follow, soon out-distance all her pursuers.

She would hide from them, and then ride home another

way, and it would be eventide before Jazr abandoned the
search and came back disconsolate, to be told that Beebee
had been home hours and hours before.

It was during one of these wild rides that Beebee had
the strange adventure I am now going to describe to you.

I myself was with her that day, and so was Miss
Morgan. This lady did not love Jazr a whit more than
did Beebee.

Miss Morgan had an exceedingly fleet horse that day,
but somehow Jazr's nag had gone lame, and Beebee rode
on ahead, quickly followed by Miss Morgan, and both
were soon far beyond the fear of any pursuit.

Instead, however, of riding homewards to-day as usual,
it pleased Beebee's fancy to turn her horse's head towards
the hills.

The poor child seemed to exult in her newly-acquired
freedom. Why should she be watched and guarded as if
she were a prisoner and a thief? she asked Miss Morgan.

" Why indeed ? " answered that lady.

" Daughters are not so treated in Merrie England, are
they, dear teacher ? "

" Oh, no, Beebee, my pupil. There they have much
freedom, and are looked upon as in every way the equals
of man ! "

" How I long to see England," said Beebee.

Then she bent down to me and patted my head.

" Some day, Shireen," she said, " some day. Ah ! I
know my freedom will come ! Perhaps my prince may
come. In all pretty stories and fairy tales a prince always
comes."

She laughed lightly as she spurred on her horse, Miss
Morgan following close to her heels.

F

But little did Beebee know that her prince had already come, and that he was at the present moment in this very forest.

"Is it not time we returned?" said Miss Morgan, after they had ridden some distance farther. "The priest's house in the wood that we passed nearly half-an-hour ago is the last in the forest. The mountains come soon now. Behold, Beebee, the pathway is already winding upwards. Farther on we may come upon the den of a wild beast, or even worse, the haunts of some evil men!"

Beebee was accustomed to be guided by her governess in everything, so she now reined up her steed, and both stopped short, and permitted the horses to help themselves to a few mouthfuls of the long tender grass that grew abundantly all around them.

The silence in this part of the dark wild forest was a silence that the heart could feel. Except for the occasional throbbing notes of a bulbul in the distance, no sound of any kind fell upon their ears for a time.

Suddenly, however, from an adjoining thicket came a sound that caused the hearts of both young ladies to beat faster as they listened breathlessly.

Twice or thrice it was repeated.

"What can it be, Miss Morgan?" said Beebee, turning a shade paler. "It sounds like someone moaning in pain or dying agony."

"Nay, nay, dear pupil," answered Miss Morgan, "we must not think that. It is in all probability but the mournful croodling of some wood pigeon. Hark, there it is again."

Once more they listened.

There could be no mistake about it now, for not only

was this moaning repeated, but after it a voice was heard calling feebly for help.

"Oh, sister," cried Beebee, now thoroughly alarmed, 'it is some poor wounded man. We cannot leave him. We must fly to his assistance."

Without adding another word Beebee pushed the branches aside and urged on her steed towards the spot from which the sounds proceeded.

Miss Morgan followed close behind.

And soon they came to a kind of green grassy glade in the forest, which, from the trampled condition of the sward, gave evidence that a fearful struggle had taken place there but very recently.

One man lay face downwards on the ground, and it was easy to see he would never need help again.

But the other, evidently an Englishman, sat half up leaning on one elbow, his other hand pressed against his side, and blood trickling over his fingers.

Beebee quickly alighted from her horse and tied the bridle to a tree.

She was a Persian, it is true, but she had a woman's heart, and here was a fellow-creature in pain and probably dying. She did not even notice that her veil had fallen down as she quickly rushed towards the stranger and knelt pityingly at his side.

CHAPTER IX.

THE ADVENTURE IN THE FOREST.

"YOU are wounded, poor stranger," cried Beebee compassionately. "Are you much hurt?" She spoke in English.

"I fear I am a little," was the faint reply. "They have attacked and robbed me, and they have slain my faithful servant, and, indeed, they left me here for dead."

"But pray," he continued, "save yourselves, young ladies. The bandits may quickly come again."

This was no time for false modesty. The poor fellow was bleeding to death. But Miss Morgan had that which no English man or woman should be without. She possessed a little skill in surgery.

So with her own handkerchief, and that of Beebee's, she quickly staunched the bleeding, then commanded her patient to lie flat upon the grass in order to lessen the force of the circulation.

"And now," said Beebee, "what are we to do? We cannot take this poor stranger to the palace. Jazr would kill him, and father would kill me."

Here Beebee blushingly restored her veil to its place.

"But," she continued, "we cannot leave him thus to

perish here in the wilderness. I have it, dear governess. Ride back quickly, and at once, to the house of the priest, and cause him to send immediately his servants with a litter. At the priest's house the stranger will be safe, and the good priest himself will be well rewarded."

" But, Beebee, my dear pupil, will you not be afraid ? "

" No, no, no," cried Beebee, and at that moment I thought my little mistress looked all a queen. She spoke to Miss Morgan impatiently, almost imperiously.

" Go immediately," she cried, " ride as hard as you safely can. Do not fear for me. I shall be safe until you return."

Next minute Miss Morgan mounted her horse and quickly disappeared.

The stranger seemed slightly better now, that he was no longer losing blood, and would have tried to sit up in order to talk, but Beebee held up a warning finger.

" You must rest," she said. " Miss Morgan would be displeased were you to sit up."

He obeyed as if he had been a child.

Although pale and sickly-looking with the loss of blood, very handsome indeed was this stranger, dark brown hair cut short, a dark moustache, well-chiselled features, and beautiful eyes, quite as blue as mine, Warlock.

" You have saved my life," he murmured. " May I ask whom I have to thank, and who is Miss Morgan ? "

" I am the only daughter of an officer of the Shah," said Beebee. " I have no mother. I may say I have no father. He—he is travelling now to Europe with our great king. Miss Morgan is the dearest friend I have on earth ; an English lady who came to me as a companion, and to teach me your beautiful language."

" You speak it well, Miss—"

"They simply call me Beebee."

"May God bless and keep you, Beebee, for ever and aye. You have to-day saved my life, and I feel very grateful. A soldier should ever be ready to die. But if he is doomed to be slain he should fall in battle, with his back to the field and his feet to the foe, and not by the hand of wretched bandits, who stab men to death for a few handfuls of gold."

"You are a soldier then? But you wear no uniform? You carry no arms?"

The wounded officer smiled feebly.

"I have been travelling for my health in your lovely country. It is not usual for British soldiers to wear uniforms or carry swords when not on duty."

"And your name, brave soldier?"

"How know you I am brave?"

"You must be brave," said Beebee innocently and naïvely, "because you are handsome, nay, even as beautiful as my father. Yes, you are brave, Mr.—"

"My name is Edgar."

"It is a strange name, but somewhat musical. Edgar, I shall often think of you. I may even dream of you, but I shall dream of you and think of you as you must appear in battle leading on your men to storm a breach. But now, talk no longer lest you faint with weakness."

"One question more, lady. You are going to have me taken to the house of a priest. But where do you yourself dwell?"

"Oh, many miles from here."

"But will you never come to see me? My wounds may take many weeks to heal."

"I do not know."

Beebee's eyes were downcast now. She was petting and smoothing my head, Warlock.

"I shall die if you do not come sometimes to see me."

"I shall send Miss Morgan, she is English."

"I will die if you do not accompany her."

"Then you must live. Oh, I would not have you die on any account. Now, be still. See, I have a little book of English poems. This is 'The Lady of the Lake.' I will read to you."

Beebee sat herself innocently down on the grass close beside the wounded stranger, and in her sweet musical young voice commenced to read that romantic and spirited poem, while Edgar listened, his eyes on her face, or on the portion of it visible.

She read on and on and on, and the time flew quietly, quickly past.

Presently, however, her quick ears detected the sound of horses' hoofs, soft though their footfall was upon the long greensward.

"They come," she cried, rising, and just at that moment the boughs were dashed aside, and Miss Morgan entered the glade, speedily followed by four or five men bearing a litter. The priest himself was with them.

"Ah!" he said in French, "one poor fellow has had his *coup de grace*. He has gone, I trust, to a better world than this; but you, Monsieur—"

He bent down and felt Edgar's pulse, long and anxiously.

A finely-formed man was this French Catholic priest. Very tall, brown with the sun, and bearded.

"You will live," he said. "You have youth and strength, and you shall have rest and quiet. All will combine to restore you."

"Thank Heaven," said Beebee.

She was bending down over me, and I noticed that she was weeping. I licked her hand, and she then took me up and embraced me.

Very gently indeed was the wounded stranger placed on that litter of soft green boughs and borne away, to the priest's house.

This house was on the edge of the forest, built on a green brae-land at the head of a bushy dell or glen, adown which went a silver thread of a river winding in and winding out among its green banks, and forming many a rapid and cascade ere it finally disappeared and rolled on in its search for the sea.

Edgar was surprised at the comfort and even elegance of everything about the French Catholic priest's house, and that evening, as the good man sat by his bedside, he took occasion to express his wonderment in as delicate language as he could command.

"You think it strange that I should dwell here almost alone. Ah! but, dear sir, I have a mission. I fill a niche. I think I even do good, and have taught souls to find Christ. The present Shah is tolerant of religions not his own, else would I soon be banished.

"You were surprised also, dear young sir," he continued, "at the deftness with which I bound up your wound and dressed your bruises, but I was not always a priest. I was a surgeon. But I loved and I lost. Oh, it is a common story enough. Then I joined the priesthood and came here an exile, and almost a hermit, to cure souls and bodies. Yes, many seek my assistance, and I never refuse it. But, believe me, my dear sir, I can be just, as well as generous, and the scoundrels who attacked you and so

basely murdered your servant shall not go unpunished.
And now, my friend, go to sleep. You have nothing to do
but get well."

Edgar was in a burning fever next day nevertheless,
and for nearly two weeks lay in bed hovering betwixt death
and life.

When he recovered sufficiently to look about him, one
beautiful afternoon, the evening sunshine stealing in through
his window and falling on a bouquet of flowers beside
him on the table, the first face he recognized was that of
Miss Morgan.

She sat not far off, quietly embroidering a piece of work.

Seeing him awake and sensible, she approached his pillow
smiling, and held something to his lips, which he swallowed
without a murmur.

"How good you have been, dear Miss Morgan!" he
murmured. "You have been near to me all the time.
No, I have not been quite insensible. And Beebee, was
she not here also?"

"She was. Sometimes. I myself have only come to see
you now and then. We—we had a difficulty in getting
away."

"How good! How good! But the difficulty?"

"It is in the fact," said Miss Morgan mournfully, "that
my sweet young friend and pupil is sold to the Shah."

"Sold to the Shah!" cried Edgar. "She, a mere child,
so beautiful, so winning! Oh, Miss Morgan, I have dreamt
of her every hour, and indeed—I—I—have got to love
her. And she is gone. Oh, how horrible!"

"Nay, nay, you misunderstand me somewhat. Beebee
has not gone. She is but promised to the Sultan or King.
When she comes of age, or rather when she is two years

older, then—she will be a slave indeed. Oh, I assure you, sir, it breaks my heart to lose her."

At this moment the door quietly opened, and Beebee herself entered, followed by the priest-physician. She started slightly when she noticed that Edgar was now awake and sensible.

He held out his hand. It was a very thin and a very white one.

"I know all, Beebee," he said. "I cannot thank you enough for your kindness, and you have come to me at great risk too. I understand what that risk has been, and I understand also Persian laws and Persian fathers. You have risked your honour and your life."

"I could not help coming," said Beebee innocently, "because I thought you would die. But now, we must part. We must never meet again. It is fate."

"Must it, indeed, be so?" said Edgar gloomily.

"Indeed, I fear it must," put in Miss Morgan.

"And I," said Edgar. "I—am a soldier. I must try not to repine. But I cannot bear to think that we shall never meet again. I will pray that it may be otherwise, and that there may be happy days yet in store for you, Beebee—may I even say for *us*."

He paused for a moment.

Beebee was silent, and weeping quietly as women-folks do, Warlock.

I had jumped up on the couch where poor Edgar lay, and was rubbing my head against his shoulder.

"This cat, Beebee," continued Edgar, "is she very dear to you?"

"She is a friend Poor Shireen! Sometimes when I am solitary and alone her affection and kindness is a great solace to me. But she is very young."

She had drawn closer to the couch, and was patting my head.

"I think she loves me," she added.

"I think," said Edgar, touching her hand lightly, "this puss, Shireen, is a medium. Else how could you have read my thoughts?"

"Shireen is yours."

"But I dare not deprive you of a friend so good and beautiful."

"Nay, nay, do not speak thus. She will be a soldier's cat."

"On one condition only shall I accept the gift, Beebee."

"And that condition?"

"That I may be permitted to bring her back to you at some future time. Within two years, Beebee?"

Once more he touched her hand.

"Two years," she said, as if speaking to herself. "I will be dead ere then."

"Nay, nay, nay," he cried, almost fiercely, "for the wrong that your parents would do you must never be accomplished."

"Speak no more, sir. Speak no more, Edgar."

"Adieu, Edgar. Adieu, Shireen."

"Adieu!"

Then they led her weeping away.

Did I ever see my sweet mistress again? Was that what you asked me, Warlock? Well, I will tell you another day. For see, my master is getting up to go. No, Vee-Vee, I do not want your convoy. Go home with master, and you, too, Dick and Warlock.

*   *   *   *   *   *

"Well, good afternoon, old friend," said Colonel Clarkson, shaking hands with Uncle Ben. " You'll come up to-morrow evening to the Castle, won't you ? "

" That will I.   Ha, your old puss is off then."

" Yes," said the Colonel. " She has queer ways altogether. She is going now on a round of visits.   I do wish she were not so old.   We shall all miss poor Shireen when she dies. Good-day."

Dick at once flew on to his master's shoulder.   Tabby cocked her tail and trotted along by his side, and the dogs followed.

It may seem strange to some readers that a starling should become so tame, but I wish the reader to remember that Dick is a study from the real life, and not a bird of the author's imagination.

The road homewards was about two miles in all.   During the walk Dick kept on his master's shoulder until about half-way to the castle.   They were then between two hedges, and just beyond was a field of turnips.   Among these Dick knew right well he would find some of his favourite tit-bits, so without saying, by your leave, to his master, he flew off over the hedge.

Colonel Clarkson waited a reasonable time, but as Dick did not reappear, he bent down towards the Tabby cat and smoothed her.

" Go, find," he said.

In a moment the cat was off through the hedge.

The Colonel listened with an amused smile on his face. He knew right well what would happen.

Then he heard Dick's voice, and knew that pussy had found the truant.

" Eh ?   Eh ?   What   is   it ? "   These   are   his   very words. " Tsc, tsc, tsc! Sugar and snails! You r—r—rascal!"

Then back flew Dick to his master. Tabby herself appeared next minute, and the journey was resumed without further incident or adventure.

Meanwhile, where was Shireen?

When Shireen left Uncle Ben's bungalow, she kept along inside the railing for some time. It was about the hour at which the butcher's dog came out for his evening run, and Shireen knew right well he would be revenged on her if he possibly could, so she was determined not to give him the chance. But the coast was clear, and soon she was in the village. She trotted into the blacksmith's shop, and he had a very kindly greeting for her. Shireen was very fond of spending half-an-hour with the blacksmith. Cats like pleasant people, and he was always laughing or singing, and often beating time to his song with the hammer on a red-hot horse-shoe, while the yellow sparks flew in all directions. Besides, there was always a nice fire here, and an air of comfort in the place—to Shireen's way of thinking. She was a high-bred cat, it is true, and a cat of ancient lineage, as we know, but she was not at all aristocratic in the choice of her friends.

Shireen left the blacksmith at last, and went to see the sick child. It is strange, but true as well as strange, that cats never fail to sympathise with human beings in grief or suffering.

But little Tom Richards was better to-night, and sitting up in his chair by the fireside. He was delighted when Shireen came in, and made his mother place a saucer of milk down for her, and puss drank a little just to please the boy.

Then she permitted him to nurse her for quite a long time. Tom, child though he was, quite appreciated the value of this compliment; for although Shireen would permit a child to take her up, and even to pull her about and tease her, no grown-up person, with the exception of the Colonel and his wife, must dare to handle her.

But Shireen jumped down at last, and begged Tommy's mother to open the door to her.

" Oh, don't let pussy go yet !" pleaded the boy.

" I must, dear, I must," said his mother, "else she may not come again."

This was very true, for cats cannot bear restraint of any kind. If they are to be truly happy they must be allowed to go and come as they please.

Before going home Shireen had still another fireside to visit. And this was Emily's.

A very humble hearth indeed; but poor Emily's eyes sparkled with joy when Shireen came trotting in.

"Oh, Shireen dear, is it you?" she cried. "Oh, you beautiful good puss, and I haven't seen you since Cracker nearly killed the butcher's dog. Look, pussy, here is Cracker."

Yes, there was Cracker, sure enough, and the dog and cat at once exchanged courtesies. Had you seen them lying together in front of the fire a few minutes after this, reader, you would never again have made use of that silly phrase—a cat and dog life. Cats and dogs, if brought up together, *do* agree. It is mankind that causes them to be enemies. A dog is far too noble an animal to touch a cat, unless he has been trained to look upon her as vermin.

"You see, I'm very busy to-night, Shireen," said Emily. " Mending stockings for father. But baby is asleep, and

so I have all the evening to myself, for I have already
done my lessons."

Poor Emily! her life was a somewhat hard one. Her
mother had died but recently, and her father, who was only
a labouring man, had been left all alone with Emily and
her baby sister. All day long the child was taken care of
by a neighbour, but as soon as school was dismissed Emily
went for her, and then her work, indeed, began. Board
Schools, as a rule, are a benefit to the nation, but there are
cases when compulsory attendance falls heavy on children
and parents too.

Emily's father was sitting on the other side of the fire
smoking his humble clay.

He bent down and stroked the cat.

"Aye, pussy,' he said, "Emily *is* very busy, and the
Lord Himself knows what I should do without her. The
Lord be thankit for a good kind daughter."

So Shireen sat there nodding and singing by the fire,
until she sang herself asleep. But when Emily arose at
last, she asked to go, and her request was immediately
granted.

"Good-night, pussy," said Emily. "Mind to come
again."

And while pussy went trotting homewards through the
darkness of a starless autumn night, Emily went in to
prepare her father's supper.

No, it is true, Emily was not a very good-looking girl,
but she had a right kind heart of her own. And this is
even better than beauty.

CHAPTER X.

WE SAILED AWAY TO THE SOUTH.

ELL, children, said Shireen, a few nights after, when she and her friends were once more all around the low and cheerful fire, the Colonel as usual in his place by the table, and Uncle Ben, cockatoo on shoulder, in an easy chair. Well, children, here we are as cosy as cosy can be; and when I see you all beside me, and the fire blinking and burning so cheerily, I feel so happy all over that I can hardly express myself, even in song.

"But hear how the wind is howling to-night!" said Tabby, looking towards the window.

"Tse, tse, tse!" said Dick, as if much impressed.

Warlock simply sat on one end, looking thoughtfully into the fire. Wind or weather did not trouble Warlock much. He was as much at home among the heather on a wild winter's day with the snow two feet deep, and clouds of ice-dust blowing, as he was among the wild flowers in dingle, dell, or forest, when summer was in its prime.

The truth is, Warlock was one of Scotland's own dogs, and these you know, are as hardy as the hills.

It was concerning this same doggie, Warlock, that the author once wrote the following lines. They were in answer to a Highland friend, who enquired through the medium of a well-known journal, if he knew the Aberdeen terrier. The verses are truly descriptive of this brave breed of dog, whether they possess any other merit or not is very little matter.

WARLOCK.

I ken the Terrier o' the North,
　　I ken the towsy tyke ;
Ye'll search frae Tweed to Sussex shore,
　　But never find his like.

For pluck and pith, and jaws and teeth,
　　And hair like heather cowes* ;
Wi' body lang and low, and strang,
　　At hame on cairns† and knowes.

He'll face a foumart‡, draw a brock‖,
　　Kill rats and whitterits§ by the score ;
He'll bang tod-lowrie¶ frae his hole,
　　Or fight him at his door.

He'll range for days and ne'er be tired,
　　O'er mountain, moor, or fell ;
Fair-play, I think, the dear wee chap
　　Would fecht the deil himsel'.

---

* Stems.　　† Heaps of stone and rubbish.　　‡ Polecat.　　‖ Badger.
§ Weasels.　　¶ The fox.

G

And yet beneath his rugged coat,
　A heart beats warm and true ;
He'll help to herd the sheep and kye,
　And mind the lammies* too.

Then see him at the ingle side,
　Wi' bairnies round him laughin' ;
Was ever dog sae pleased as he,
　Sae fond o' fun and daffin ? †

But gie's your han', my Hielan man,
　In troth ! we manna sever ;
Then here's to Scotia's best o' dogs,
　Our towsy‡ tyke for ever.

On this particular evening Warlock's boots were somewhat muddy. Tabby's had also been the same, though
she had taken pains to clean them before coming to the
fireside. The muddiness of their boots, however, only
pointed to the fact that the two friends had enjoyed a
rare day's sport in the woods, or by the water's side.

Well, said Shireen, as to the wind, I do not dislike
hearing it, when I am indoors, nor hearing the rain
rattling against the window panes either. I always think
the fire burns brighter on a night like this. Besides, the
howling and howthering of the storm carries my thoughts
back to the golden days of my youth, and to the events
of my life at sea.

Shireen paused for a moment with one snow-white paw
raised thoughtfully in the air.

"Warlock," she said, next minute, "what do you see in
the fire ?"

"Me ?" said Warlock, rousing himself out of his reverie.

---

* Young lambs.　　† Joking.　　‡ Rough and unkempt in coat.

"Me, Shireen? Oh, I see a water-rat's hole down under the banks of a dark brown stream, and I can see the water-rats pop in and out. There, look, I see one now standing on end at the other side of the bank, rubbing the water out of his eyes with the back of his knuckles, the better to look over at me and Tabby."

"What do you see, Mother Shireen?" said Vee-Vee.

I see a ship, my son, tossing hither and thither on the far-off Indian Ocean. I see the waves breaking in snowy spray, high, high against her jet-black sides. I see the racing waves curling their angry crests as they roll on towards the rugged horizon. I see dark storm clouds sweeping swift across the sky, with rifts of blue between, through which pours now and then a glint of sunshine.

"Mother Shireen, you were on that ship?" said Tabby, "tell us."

Yes, Tabby, I was on that ship. And dear master too. Last evening I told you how my sweet little mistress Beebee, had given me away to the wounded officer before she bade him adieu.

I was vexed to lose her. I would, I thought, never, never see my old home again; never more lie on summer evenings on the turret balcony, watching with Beebee the sunlight and shade chasing each other across the dreamy woods, and the birds wheeling far beneath us in giddy flight. When Beebee had really gone, I scarce could believe that we were parted. I could not realise my loss at first. I went to the door and mewed, I jumped up into the window-sill, and examined the fastening of the jalousies.

"Shireen, come to me. Come, puss, come."

I looked quickly around, and my eyes fell on the face of the soldier Edgar.

He looked wan and worn and old. Though but little
more than six-and-twenty, and that is young for a man, he
appeared to me in his grief and loneliness to be about
sixty.

My heart went out to him at once. Oh, Tabby, I do
believe that if human beings would only bear in mind, how
sickness or helplessness in one of their race appeals to us
poor cats, and how we love the feeble, the ill, and the old,
as well as dear children, they would often be kinder to us.
But this is a digression.

I jumped down from the window, and with a fond cry
leapt up on the couch where soldier Edgar lay.

I was singing now.

I have often observed that the song of a cat seems to
soothe a human being's soul and calm his nerves, continued
Shireen. Well, I had a duty to perform to this poor sick
soldier, and I was determined to do it.

What is duty, did you ask, Warlock? Well, it is a
word I have borrowed from the human race. It means
the doing of that which you have been told off to do, and
that it is your business to do. Strangely enough human
beings usually want to be preached at before they can
tackle their duty—if I may be excused for talking
sailor fashion—while we cats and dogs, yes, and birds,
Dick, feel impelled to duty by our own instincts only.
But I had already become fond of soldier Edgar, because I
knew my mistress liked him.

"Shireen," he said, smoothing me but smiling, "you
must not mourn too much for your mistress. She is not
gone quite away, because she dwells here in my heart,
Shireen. So we will often think of her together. I will
love you for her sake, and you will love me for her sake.

That is mutuality, pussy, so there! Now sit by me and
sing, and I will sleep and awake calm and refreshed. I
want to get better soon now, Shireen, because I intend
coming back here again if possible, and take Beebee your
mistress away. I want to save her from a fearful doom."

* * *

I hardly know how the time passed after this for a
month, during which time new master and I lived in the
house of the priest.

But by this time master was strong and well again.
Then came the day of parting.

The priest rode with us a very long way through the
forest, and told us which way was the nearest to the city.
Then we said—Farewell.

But the priest's last words as he held Edgar's hand were
these: "If it be in my power to prevent it, my friend,
depend upon it Beebee shall never enter the palace of the
Shah!"

" May Heaven bless you," said the soldier. He said no
more. I do not think he could have done so had he tried,
for tears seemed to rise and choke him.

Well, the next thing I distinctly remember, is being
taken on board a man-o'-war ship from a boat that left
the Apollo Bunder at Bombay.

I had one regret just then, for my thoughts reverted to
Beebee in her turret chamber. I imagined her sitting
there all alone with Miss Morgan, and gazing dreamily
over the sea, the sea she so longed to float upon.

But once on board the ship I had little time to think
very much, at first at all events. Everything was very

new and very strange to me; and it would take me some time to get up to the ropes, you know, Warlock.

"Oh!" said Warlock, "we dogs don't bother about ropes. When we come to a new home or house we just settle down there. All we want to know is where the door is."

Ah! Warlock, yes, that I know is true. But think how different a dog's life is from that of a poor cat. We cats have got to be wise, Warlock, and we've got to be wily, for though we have not got the brand of Cain upon our brows, still almost everybody who meets us wants to kill us.

It was on this very subject that only last Sunday I was conversing with the parson's big tom-cat.

"I'm so much used to travelling now, Tom," I said, "having had a spell of over twenty years of it, that I don't mind where I go; but if I were not a travelling cat I should feel very much from home in a new house, not knowing the outs and ins of it, the upstairs and the down, and where to get food, where to watch for mice, and the drains to run into when the school children come past; or the trees to run up when the butcher's dog comes round the corner."

"Well, for many reasons," said Tom in answer, "I like dogs well enough. But I wouldn't like to be a dog, mind you, Shireen. Now look at me for example. I am the parson's cat to be sure, and being a parson's cat people might think I was under some restrictions. Not a bit of it, Shireen. I'm my own master.

"Now, look for example, at the Saint Bernard dog Dumpling—an honest contented great fellow he is—but bless you, Shireen, he isn't free. But I am. Dumpling can't do what he pleases—I can. I can go to bed when I like, rise when I like, and eat and drink when, where, and what I choose. Dumpling *can't*. Really, Shireen, my old friend, I can forgive Dumpling for chasing me into the apple tree last Sunday, when I think of the dull life a dog leads, and how few are his joys compared to mine. Poor Dumpling needs the servants to wait upon him. He can't walk a couple of miles by himself and be sure of finding his way back, or sure of not getting into a row, getting stolen, or some other accident equally ridiculous.

"The other day, Shireen, if you'll take my word for it, Dumpling actually sat on the doorstep for two hours in the pouring, pitiless rain till his great shaggy coat was soaked to the skin, because, forsooth, he didn't know how to get the door opened. Would a cat have done that? No, a cat would have walked politely up to the first kind-faced passenger that came along and asked him to be good enough to ring the bell, and the thing would have been done. Could Dumpling unlatch a door or catch a mouse? Not to save his life. Could he climb a tree and examine a sparrow's nest? Not he. Could he find his way home over the tiles on a dark night? A pretty figure he would cut if he were only going to try. No, Shireen, dogs have their uses, but they're not in the same standard with cats."

Well, Warlock, mind these are Tom's views and not mine : but as I was telling you all, I found myself safe on board the *Venom* at last, and that same afternoon we sailed away to the south.

Master being still somewhat of an invalid, the doctor had given him and me the use of his cabin, he himself sleeping at night inside a canvas screen on the main deck.

The *Venom*, I must tell you, wasn't a very large ship, and she was engaged in what fighting human-sailors called the suppression of the slave trade. Not that I meant to trouble my head very much about any such nonsense, only in one way it appealed to us ; it would make our passage down to the far-off Cape of Good Hope and so home to England a very much longer one.

"You see," the captain said to my soldier Edgar on the quarter-deck the first day, "we are awfully glad to have you with us, but we can't hurry even on your account."

"I wouldn't wish you to do so,' Captain Beecroft. The long voyage will do me a wonderful deal of good ; besides I don't really long to be home. I'd rather be back in Persia again."

The captain looked at him somewhat searchingly and smiled.

I was walking up and down with the pair of them, with my tail in the air and looking very contented and pleased, because the sun was shining so brightly, and the ocean, which I could catch peeps at through the port-holes, was as blue as *lapis lazuli.*

"I say," said the captain, "did you lose your heart out there ?"

"I did," was the reply. "Oh, I am ten years older than Beebee, and perhaps more, and nothing may ever come of it. But, sir, she saved my life."

"Do you see this cat ?" he continued, taking me up in his arms. "Well, this is Shireen. The girl who so bravely saved my life gave Shireen to me.'

"Wait a minute," said Captain Beecroft. "Come into my cabin here. Now sit down and just tell me all the story."

Edgar did so, and I think that from that moment these two men were fast friends.

My master also showed the captain the beautiful little ruby that was set in my tooth.

" A strange notion!" said the latter.

" It is not an uncommon one among eastern ladies," said the soldier. "Anyhow," he added, "I should always know Shireen again if I happened to lose her, and she returned even ten years after."

Somehow, my children, those words, simple though they were, had an ominous ring in them, and I thought of them long, long after, in far less happy times.

Well, Warlock, after I had been a few days at sea, I determined to get up to the ropes. I must see everything there was to be seen, for as far as I had yet noticed, there was nothing to be very greatly afraid of.

But I resolved to make my first excursion round the ship by night.

So soon after sunset I went quietly upstairs, and immediately found myself under the stars on deck.

CHAPTER XI.

S soon as I got on deck I began to glance eagerly about me.

The moon was shining very brightly, and the waves all the way to the horizon were stippled with light, while the bright stars were reflected and multiplied in the water like a myriad of diamonds.

There was a breeze blowing just then, so there was no need for the present to keep steam up, as a sailor calls it.

Steam is not nice on board ship, Warlock. There is a terrible noise, and everywhere the ship is shaken. You cannot help fancying you are inside a mill all the time, with such a multitude of wheels rattling round and round, that it quite bewilders one.

But to-night there was hardly a hush on deck, except now and then the trampling of the sailors' feet, or a song borne aft from the forecastle.

I was not a ship's cat yet, you know, Warlock, and so didn't know the names of things. But I soon found a guide, or rather the guide found me. I was standing on the quarter-deck, as it is called, looking about me in a very

uncertain kind of way, when I heard soft footsteps stealing
up behind me, and, looking round, was rather startled to
see standing there in the moonlight, which made him look
double the size, an immense black Thomas cat, with yellow
fiery eyes.

I was going to bolt down the stairs again at once, and
ask my master to come and shoot him, but there was a
sort of music in his voice which appealed to me the
moment he spoke.

"Oh, you lovely, angelic pussy princess," he said ; "be not
afraid, I pray you. Hurry not away, for if you leave the
deck the moon will cease to shine, and the stars will lose
their radiance."

He advanced stealthily towards me as he spoke, singing
aloud. But I sprang upon the skylight at once, raised my
back and growled, as much probably in terror as in anger.

"Come but one step nearer," I cried, "and I will leap
into the foaming sea."

"Dear princess," he said, "I would rather lose my life.
I would rather throw my body to the sharks than any ill
should happen to a hair of your head."

"See," he continued, jumping on the top of a kind of
wooden fence, which sailors call the bulwarks, that ran
round, what I then called the lid (deck) of the ship. "See!
speak the word, and I shall rid you for ever of my hateful
presence ! "

I was very much afraid then.

I did not want to see this Thomas cat drowned before
my eyes, for although he was very black, I could not help
noticing that he was comely.

"Oh," I cried, "come down from off that fearful fence
and I will forgive you, perhaps even take you into favour."

Well, Warlock, strange though it may appear, in three minutes' time this Thomas cat and I were as good friends as if we had known each other for years.

"You are very lovely," he said. "Strange how extremes meet, for I have been told that I am quite ugly. Your coat is snow-white, mine is like the raven's wing. Your fur is long and soft and silky, my hair is short and rough, and there are brown holes burned in it here and there, where sailors have dropped the ashes from their pipes. You are doubtless as spotless in character as you are in coat; but—well, Shireen, the cook has sometimes hinted to me that as far as my ethics are concerned I—I am not strictly honest. Sometimes the cook has hinted that to me by word of mouth, at other times, Shireen, with a wooden ladle."

"But come," he added, "let me show you round the ship."

"May I ask your name," I said; "you already know mine?"

"My name is Tom."

"A very uncommon name, I daresay."

"Well—yaas. But there *are* a few English cats of that name, as you may yet find out. My last name is Brandy. Tom Brandy,* there you have it all complete. Sounds nice, doesn't it?"

"It does, indeed. Has it any meaning attached to it?"

"Well, then, it has. Brandy is a kind of fluid that some sailors swallow when they go on shore. They have often tried to make me take some, but I never would with my free will. It turns men into fiends, Shireen. For in a

---

* Tom Brandy is a sketch from the life.

short time after they swallow it they appear to be excellent
fellows, and they sing songs and shake hands, and vow to
each other vows of undying love and affection. But soon
after that they quarrel and fight most fiercely, and often
take each other's lives, as I have known them to do in the
camps among the miners out in Australia, where I was
born."

"Oh, have you been in a real mine, Tom ? "

" Yes, I first opened my eyes at the diggings."

" Oh, how lovely ! Was it at Golconda. I have heard
Beebee, my mistress, read about Golconda in a book. And
were there rubies and diamonds and amethysts all lying
about, and gold and silver ? "

" Not much of that, Shireen. My bed was a grimy old
coat, belonging to one of the miners. My home was a wet
and dark slimy hole, and the miners were not very romantic.
They were as rough as rough could be. Any sailor you see
here would look like a prince beside a miner. But though
as rough as any of them, my master, a tall red man, with
a long red beard, was kind-hearted, and for his sake I
stayed in camp longer than I would otherwise have done.

"When I was old enough to catch my first rat the
miners crowded round me, and said they would baptize
me in *aguardiente ;* that was the fiery stuff they were
drinking, and so they did. Some of it got into my eyes
and hurt them very much. That is how I was called Tom
Brandy.

" Another day, when I was grown up, they forced some
spoonfuls of brandy and water down my throat, and by-and-
bye I seemed to get out of my mind. I walked round the
camp and challenged every other he cat in the place, and
fought almost as bad as a miner.

" I was always death on dogs, Shireen, but that night there wasn't a dog anywhere about that I did not try to swallow alive, for I believed myself to be as big as an elephant. My master found me at last, and kindly took me home and laid me on his old coat in the corner, and I soon fell sound asleep, but, oh, Shireen, when I awoke next day my head and eyes were fit to burst with pain.

" Then, by-and-bye, there came a parson to our camp, and my master would walk miles to hear the preaching, and I always went with him. When there were many dogs about master used to lead me with a string, but he never chained me up in his house, as some miners did with their big cats. It is cruel to chain a dog even, but much more cruel to chain a cat.

" Well, master was what they call a rolling stone ; one of the sort that don't gather moss, you know. So he often changed camp. It took us two days and nights sometimes to get to the new camp, and I travelled all the way in an old gin case.

" Poor master ! "

" Did he die ? " said I.

" Well, it was like this. Often and often on lovely moonlit nights, Shireen, master and I would sit in the door of the hut where he lived out among the bush and scrub, and he would speak to me of his far-off home in England, and of his young wife and children that he was trying to dig gold for.

" ' It is that,' he told me once, ' which makes me so restless, Tom. I want to get money. I want to get home to them, pussy, and I'll take you with me and we'll be so happy.'

" And he would smooth my head and sing to me of the

happy time that was coming when we should get home
with wealth and riches.

"'When the wild wintry wind
Idly raves round our dwelling,
And the roar of the linn*
On the night breeze is swelling ;
So merrily we'll sing,
As the storm rattles o'er us,
Till the dear shieling † ring
With the light lilting chorus.'"

"But, ah! Shireen, that happy time never came, for one
sad night, at the stores, a quarrel arose about something,
and next moment the noise of pistol-shooting rang out
high above the din of voices.

"There was a moment or two of intense stillness, and
my master fell back into the arms of a friend.

"'Oh, my dear wife and bairns!' That was all master
had breath to say before his death-blood rose and choked
him.

"They told me I nearly went wild with grief, that I
jumped upon his breast and cried and howled. Well,
perhaps I did. I forget most of what happened. Only I
know they buried him next day, and I sat on the grave
for days, refusing to leave it. Then I wandered off to
Melbourne. I thought if I could only get home and find
master's wife, and children, I might be a comfort to them.
But this was impossible.

"Well, I stayed for some months in Melbourne, just a
waif and a stray, you know, begging my bread from door
to door. Then the *Venom*, the very ship we are now on,

* A cataract or rapid.   † A cottage.

Shireen, lay in, and when walking one night near the docks, a sailor came singing along the street. He looked so good and so brown and so jolly that my heart went out to him at once, and I spoke to him.

"'Hullo!' he cried, 'what a fine lump of a cat. Why, you *are* thin though, Tom.'"

" How did he know your name? " said I.

" Oh, just guessed it, I suppose.

"'How thin you are!' he says. 'Well, on board you goes with me, and you shall be our ship's cat, and if any man Jack bullies you, why they'll have to fight Bill Bobstay.' And that is how I came to be a ship's cat, my lovely Shireen."

" Nobody objected to your being on board, I suppose," said I.

" Well, I don't know, for you see, next day was Sunday, and seeing they were rigging up a church on the main deck, I went and sat down by the parson very demure-like, as I had sat beside poor master in the miners' camp.

"Then, after church, the first lieutenant asked the men, who brought the cat on board. But of course nobody knew.

"'Throw him overboard,' cried the lieutenant.

"'No, no,' said the captain. 'That will never do, Mr. Jones. The poor cat is welcome to his bite and sup as long as he likes to stop with us, whoever brought him on board.'

" Then a man in the ranks saluted.

"'Did you want to say anything?' said Captain Beecroft.

"'Well, sir,' said the man, 'I wouldn't like any of my pals to be blamed for a-bringing of Tom from shore, 'cause *I* did, and you may flog me if you like.'

" 'No, no, my man, instead of flogging you I'll forgive you. I like my men to be bold and outspoken just as you are.'

" And from that day to this, three long years, Shireen, I've been ship's cat to the saucy *Venom*, and, what is more, I like it.

" Now, if you please, I'll take you forward, and you can see the men's quarters."

" What are those three trees growing on the lid of the ship for, Tom?" I asked.

" Those are not trees, Shireen," he answered ; " those are what they call ship's masts, and you must not say the lid of the ship, but the deck."

" Thank you, Tom. And are those sheets hung up yonder to dry, Tom?"

" Oh, no, those are the ship's sails. They carry the vessel along before the wind when the steam isn't up. Look down into that hole, Shireen. Take care you don't fall. Do you see all those clear glittering shafts and cranks and things? Well, those are the engines. Keep well away from them when they begin to move, else you might tumble in and be killed in a moment."

" How strange and terrible !" I said.

Well, children, Tom took me everywhere all over the ship, and even introduced me to the men.

" My eyes, Bill," said one man, " here's a beauty. Did you ever see the like of her before? White's the snow ; long coat and eyes like a forget-me-not. Stand well back, Bill. Don't smoke over her. She belongs to that soldier officer, and I'll warrant he wouldn't like a hole burned in that beautiful jacket she wears."   .

But oh, children, for many weeks I thought ship-life was

II

about the most awkward thing out, for when it isn't blowing
enough to send the vessel on through the water, then, you
know, they start the mill and the rattling wheels, and your
poor life is nearly shaken out of you, while the blacks keep
falling all about, and if a lady has a white coat like mine,
why—why it won't bear thinking about. And if it does
blow, Warlock, well, then it is too awkward for anything,
and sometimes it was about all Tom Brandy could do to
hang out, although his claws were sharper and stronger far
than mine.

But long before we reached the city of Zanzibar I was,
I think, quite as good a ship's cat as Tom Brandy himself.

I'll never forget, however, the first day Tom took me
aloft.

We went as far as the maintop, and there we sat together
talking for quite an hour.

"Hullo!" said Tom at last, "there goes eight bells and
the bugle for dinner; come on, Shireen."

Tom began to go down at once, but lo! when I looked
over my heart grew faint and my head felt giddy, and I
wouldn't have ventured after Tom for anything.

"No, no, Tom," I cried, "save yourself. Never mind me."

"Why, there is no danger," he answered. "Only you
mustn't try it head first as if you were coming out of a
tree, but hand after hand, thus."

And Tom soon disappeared.

I sat there till the shades of evening began to fall. Tom,
however, hadn't quite forgotten me, for he brought me up
the breast of a chicken.

After I had partaken of it: "Will you try to come
down now, Shireen?" he said.

"No, Tom," I replied. "I shall end my days up
here. I—"

SITTING ON THE CROSSTREES.

I said no more. For at that moment a rough red face appeared over the top.

It was the honest sailor-man who had brought Tom Brandy on board, and he soon solved the difficulty by taking me down under his arm.

But I gained confidence after this, and was soon able to run up even to the top-gallant crosstrees, and come down again feet first, and hand after hand, just like Tom Brandy himself.

I'll never forget the first day I heard the guns go off. Tom told me it was nothing. That we were merely chasing a slave-ship, and that the moment she lay to our brave sailors would board her, and very soon make an end of the Arabs.

Tom and I had crept into the largest gun that day, having found the tompion out. She was called a bow-chaser, whatever that may be, and she stood on a pivot away forward. The sun had been fearfully hot that forenoon, but Tom came aft to the quarter-deck, where I was lying panting, with my mouth open.

"Very hot, isn't it?" said Tom.

"I feel roasting," I replied.

"Well, follow me," he said. "I know where it is dark and cool enough for anything. The tompion is out of the 56 pound-er."

"Whatever do you mean? What is a tompion, Tom? And what is a 56 pound-er?"

"Come on and see, Shireen."

Then we went to the gun.

"Follow your leader," cried Tom, and in he crawled and soon was lost to view.

"But why, Tom?" I cried; "it must be dirty as well as dark. I'm afraid of soiling my coat."

Tom looked out of the gun to laugh.

"Oh, Shireen!" he said, "the idea of a Royal Navy gun being dirty. I wonder what the gunner would say if you told him?"

So, half ashamed of myself, I jumped in. It was delightfully nice and cool, and so my companion and I fell sound asleep.

I was awakened before Tom by a voice. "Can't load the bow-chaser, sir. Cats have both gone to sleep in it, and I can't get 'em out."

"Stick in a fuse," cried the lieutenant, "and rouse them out."

Immediately after there was a rang-bang let off behind us, and Tom and I were blown clean out of the gun.

We weren't hurt, Warlock, for we both alighted on our feet; but, my blue eyes! I did get a scare.

Tom said that was nothing. He often went to sleep in the gun, and, as to being blown out with a fuse, it didn't even singe one, and was quicker than walking.

But when the battle began in earnest, and the first gun went off, I bolted aft with my tail like a bottle-brush, and dived down below.

I tore in through the ward-room, and did not consider myself safe until I got into my master's bed.

The battle didn't last long. Tom told me it was only a small slaver. But she was captured, and towed astern, and Tom said there was some talk of hanging one or two of the Arabs, but I didn't know anything about this.   I was very pleased the fight was over.

Three slaves were brought on board.   One was a little boy, with no more clothes on than a mermaid.   And he was so black, children, that when he crawled up and put his arms round my neck, I quite expected to see a black ring round me next time I looked in the glass.

But the blackness didn't come off.

Strangely enough, this poor little black child and I grew very great friends indeed.

I think that by this time, however, there wasn't an officer or man in the ship, fore or aft, that didn't love me very much.

CHAPTER XII.

OM and I, continued Shireen, weren't the only pets on board the *Venom*. There was a monkey though, and a very large one he was. When he stood up he was as big as a second-class boy. The sailors had dressed him as a marine, and given him a wooden gun, and taught him to shake hands and salute. His name was Joe; but I'm sure he wasn't happy, I often saw tears in his eyes, or thought I did. Perhaps he had been taken from his home, far away in the beautiful forests of Africa, and had left a wife and children behind him.

We had a mongoose too—a sly old grey creature that the men petted. But Tom never took to him, and used sometimes to whack him when nobody was looking.

We had a large chameleon just like Chammy,—and I wonder where Chammy is—our ship's chameleon lived in an old coffee-pot that was turned down on its side like a kennel in the corner of the doctor's cabin. He was chained to this just like a doggie, and used to catch little cockroaches and hammer-legged flies for himself all day.

In another part of the doctor's cabin was a lizard four feet long, that looked terribly fierce and dangerous. He was also secured with a chain. In a hatbox, in the doctor's cabin, lived a beautiful bronze-winged pigeon, who purred like a cat. Tom said he must be awfully good to eat, but he wouldn't venture into the cabin for anything, owing to the dragon that was chained in the corner.

We had in the wardroom a grey parrot with a red tail that he was very proud of. And all the week through the parrot was allowed to go on deck if he liked, but not on Sundays, because once when he came to church in the middle of the service he set everybody laughing by calling the parson "Old Boots."

The sailors now began to teach me tricks, and seeing that it pleased them very much, I tried to learn my lessons as quickly as possible.

On fine evenings then at smoking time, the men would call me forward, and a ring would be formed near to the winch and between the bows.

Jumping backwards and forwards over a stick, or over a man's clasped hands, was nothing. Heigho! my dear children, this happened twenty years ago, although I remember it as if it were but yesterday. Well, I was supple and strong, and lithe of limb in those dear days, being little more than a kitten, and a man could hardly hold a stick so high that I couldn't spring over it.

As soon as I was fairly well accomplished at this work, a piece of iron wire, bent in a half hoop, was used instead of the stick, and every night the sailor who was teaching me brought the two ends of the wire nearer and nearer, until at last it was a whole hoop and nothing else.

Next he covered the hoop half over with paper, leaving just a hole, but I was determined not to be beaten, and through I went.

One evening, to my surprise, the hoop was all covered with thin paper; nevertheless, when the man spoke kindly to me, and asked me to leap, through I went, and my education in leaping was supposed to be complete.

This man was afterwards called aft to the quarter-deck, and there, to the delight and amusement of the officers, and the envy of the mongoose, who couldn't jump a bit, I went through the whole performance, and was applauded sky-high.

"Pussy," said my master laughing, as he took me and fondled me in his arms, "I never knew before that you were a play actor."

＊　　＊　　＊　　＊　　＊　　＊　　＊

There were no rats on board the *Venom*, so Tom and I had an idle time of it. When Tom first came on board ship in Australia, there had been a large number of these nasty creatures in the vessel. They used to eat everything, and sometimes they got into the men's hammocks for warmth, and slept with them all throughout the watch-in. But Tom cleared the ship by degrees.

"That must have been fine fun," said Warlock; "but it must have been dull times for Tom and you—no rats, no sport."

"But," added wise, wee Warlock, with a sigh, "it will be as bad in this country, Tabby, before long."

" Yes," said Tabby.

" What I would propose if I were in Parliament," said Warlock, " would be this. We have a close season for birds, and even for seals, so we ought to have a close season for rats also."

" Bravo! Bravo! tse, tse, tse!" cried Dick.

" Then if we had a close season for rats, though the farmers might grumble a bit, Tabby and I would have sport, and it is everybody for himself in this world. But, dear Mother Shireen, we are interrupting the easy flow of your narrative. Pray go on."

Yes, Warlock, and I think if you wait for sport till a close season for rats becomes the law of the land, you'll be pretty old and stiff before you get it. But on board the saucy *Venom*, although Tom and I scorned to catch cockroaches like the big ape and the mongoose, we had fine fun at night fishing.

" Fishing?" cried Tabby. " Why, whatever did you catch, Mother Shireen? Sharks?"

No, my dear, nor whales either, though a shark once nearly caught me. No, we caught flying fish, Tom and I.

" Tse, tse, tse!" from Dick.

I observe that Dick is much surprised. Perhaps he thinks I am becoming foolish in my old age. Not a bit of it, Dick. Tom taught me how to catch the flying fish, and I soon became a very apt pupil indeed. And easy work it was. You see, flying fish instead of being chased by dolphins, though they sometimes may be, or by sharks either, are generally out in shoals, looking for their own food, and they fly, Warlock, just for the fun of the thing.

" For sport like?" said Warlock.

Yes, Warlock, for sport.

Well, they always will fly to a light, and so all Tom and I had to do was to sit on the top of the bulwarks and look down. The starlight, flashing in our eyes, soon attracted the attention of the fish, and they jumped over our heads, and danced a jig on the deck behind us.

Then Tom and I went and had a very nice little supper, and there was always more than we could eat, so the men on watch had some too.

" Well, that is good," said Tabby. " I've tried my hand at trout fishing, but I never heard of flying-fish catching like that before."

" Trout fishing," said Shireen, " is what I should call mere bottom fishing."

" Yes, and you do go to the bottom too, with a plump."
Shireen laughed.

" It may be all very well for short-haired Tabbies like you, my dear," she remarked. " But, la! to get my jacket wet would entirely spoil it; besides, you know, I'm not so young as you. If I got wet I should be laid up with the rheumatics for a month to a dead certainty. Heigho! it might be a *dead* certainty too, though that, children, is only my little joke. But tell us Tabby, how you got on fishing."

Tabby sat up for a moment, and Dick flew off her back, crying,

" I say, I say, what is it? you r—r—rascal ! "

" Well," said Tabby, " it wasn't with me that the catching of trout originated, nor with Warlock either. It happened thus. In a cottage near the forest, a year or two ago, there came an old maiden lady to live, who was very fond indeed of cats. She had three altogether, and she very wisely

permitted them to roam about at the freedom of their own
will. Two of her cats were ladies, the other was a fine red
fellow, of the name of Joe.

"The gamekeepers said that Joe was a noted thief, and
that he caught their birds and their leverets also, and that
they would shoot him on sight. When the old lady heard
this, she went straight to the keepers' huts by the forest
edge. Joe was trotting by her side, but as soon as they
were within fifty yards of the cottages, Joe got up on his
mistress's shoulder. She was a strong old lady, and armed
with a two-horse power umbrella in one hand, and a big
book in the other.

"'Do you see this cat?' said Miss Simmonds to the head
keeper.

"'Can't help seeing him, miss,' he answered, 'besides,
we know him ; he kills our birds and our leverets too, and
we've seen him take a grilse out of the river!'

"'Well, that is a pity ; I just called to say that I was
sorry, and that I will do my best to keep Joe at home,
though this is difficult sometimes with a tom-cat, you
know. But if he kills a bird or a leveret, you must let me
know the amount of damage, and I'll pay. But,' she
added, 'you must not take the law into your own hands
and shoot my cat.'

"'Nonsense, miss!' cried the keeper, pointing to a board
on which was printed :

"TRESPASSERS WILL BE PROSECUTED."

"DOGS WILL BE SHOT."

'That's the way we serves dogs, miss, and it isn't likely
we'll trouble about sparing a cat.'

"'Then Miss Simmonds stuck her big umbrella ferule down in the turf, and took the big book from under her arm.

"'Listen,' she said. 'Ahem! *Corner* v. *Champneys*. 2 Marsh, 584. A gamekeeper has no right to kill a dog for following game, even although the owner of the dog has received notice that trespassing dogs will be shot. In such a case as this, the shooter must pay the full price of the animal shot.'

"'Didn't know that before,' said the keeper. 'But, begging your pardon, miss, cats are not dogs.'

"'The same law holds good, sir.'

"'Cats can be trapped, miss.'

"'Listen again,' said Miss Simmonds. '*Townsend* v. *Witham*. In this case it was ruled that the defendant was answerable to the plaintiff for injuries sustained by his cat and dog in a trap, although he had no intention of injuring plaintiff, and meant only to catch foxes and vermin.'

"'Poison, miss, is a quiet way of getting rid of cats. I'll try that.'

"Once again, Miss Simmonds turned over the pages of her book, and proved to the satisfaction of even those surly keepers, that the putting down of poisoned flesh in a field laid the perpetrator under a penalty of £10.

"Well, although Miss Simmonds laid down the law to those men, she did not part from them in an unfriendly way, and something bright and yellow passed from her hand to that of the keeper.

"But in future Miss Simmonds restricted Joe's liberty somewhat.

"Well, one day, Warlock and I were sitting by the

burn* somewhat disconsolately, for we hadn't had
very much sport that day, only a few field mice and a
mole, when I heard a cat mew softly within a few yards
of me.

" I looked quickly round, and Warlock pricked up his
ears, and prepared for instant combat.

" It was Joe.

" And very handsome he looked. I lost my heart to him
at once.

" 'Shall I give him a fit?' said Warlock.

" 'No, no,' I cried hastily ; 'that is Joe.'

" 'I'm a little afraid of your dog, miss,' said Joe. 'Will
he bite?'

" 'Oh, no, sir,' I hastened to say.

" Then Joe advanced.

" All three soon got talking in quite a neighbourly kind
of way, and the conversation naturally enough turned upon
sport.

" 'We haven't done much this forenoon,' I said.

" 'Ah! then why don't you catch trout?'

" Just at that moment fire seemed to flash from Joe's
yellow eyes. His nose was turned towards the stream ; he
was crouching low with his tail all a-quiver. Next minute
he had left the bank and disappeared with a splash in the
water.

" I was thunderstruck. So was Warlock. But Joe crept
up the bank again almost directly, with a beautiful crimson-
dotted yellow trout in his mouth.

" This he placed at my feet as a love-offering. Then he
shook himself once or twice, and seemed quite pleased to

---

* A small stream or rivulet is so called in Scotland.

see me enjoy the trout, the head and tail of which I gave to Warlock.

"'Delightful, isn't it?' he said.

"'Delicious!' I replied.

"'I've been a fisherman for over five years. You see, my late master had always been a disciple of Walton's, and when only a kitten I used to sit and sing beside him, when packing his luncheon for the river's side. I jumped up when he took down rod and basket, and would trot off with him all the way to the river. How eagerly I used to watch the skimming fly, and my master can make a lovely cast, and I couldn't help being all of a tremble, and squaring my mouth, and emitting little screams of delight, when a fish rose to nibble; then when one was caught and thrown on the bank, nothing could prevent my jumping on it and killing it with blows of my paw. I did not put a tooth in it because master always fed me well, and I knew there was luncheon in the basket for me as well as for him.

"'But I soon learned to catch fish myself, and now I not only spring on them as you saw me do just now, but where the stream is shallow, I fish as I have seen schoolboys do; for lying down on the bank I stretch my paw far in under it, and very often hand out a trout.'

"'How clever!' I said.

"'It is wonderful!' said Warlock.

"'Well,' said Joe, 'you can do the same.'

"'Can I?' asked Warlock.

"'No,' said Joe smiling. 'You're only a dog, you know, but you can sit on a hillock, and watch and warn us if you see any fiend-boys coming along with catapults.'

"So, as Joe's late master had been a disciple of Walton's,

JOE TROUT-FISHING.

I became a disciple of Joe's. I think, Shireen, that I have proved a very apt pupil, though not quite as good yet as Joe. For Joe takes to the water like an Irish spaniel, and he told me that he often caught eels and also water rats.

"My fishing lessons have been an advantage to me and to Warlock too, because previously I used to be rather afraid of the water, and more than once when Warlock and I were out hunting, and he swam over a stream, I had to go miles up or down till I found a bridge. But now I leap in just as Warlock does, and swim to the other side."

*   *   *   *   *

Shireen got up and stretched herself now.

"I'll go on with my story another night," she said.

Then she jumped upon Colonel Clarkson's knee.

"How fond that cat seems to be of you," said Ben.

"Ah! yes, poor Shireen! She dearly loves both me and my wife. As for Lizzie and Tom, well, she adores them. But Tom here is such a good lad, and never pulls her about, for I have told him that pussy is very old, and, heigho! I daresay we'll miss her some of these days."

"But we can lift Tabby, can't we, uncle?" said Lizzie.

"Well, I do think Tabby rather likes being teased just a very little, and I'm sure she would stand from you, Lizzie, treatment she would soon resent if Uncle Ben or I were going to resort to it."

"Getting late," said Uncle Ben, starting up. "But," he added, "somehow when the wind roars as it does to-night, and takes my thoughts away back to the stormy ocean, I cannot help talking."

"Won't Cockie get wet?" said Mrs. Clarkson. "Hadn't you better leave him here to-night?"

"Bless your innocence, my dear Mrs. Clarkson, the bird would break his heart."

"Coakie wants to go home!" cried the cockatoo.

It will be observed that the bird called himself *Coakie*, not Cockie.

But Ben produced a big red handkerchief, and simply tied Cockie up as if he had been a bundle of collars going to the wash.

He placed the bundle under his arm, bade everybody good-night, then walked boldly forth into darkness and storm.

CHAPTER XIII.

"AWAY, LIFEBOAT'S CREW!"

HE house where the Clarksons dwelt, with the two dear little orphans Lizzie and Tom, and to which Uncle Ben so often found his way, was a fine old place. It stood high on a great green brae, not far from the forest and sea, and had been at one time a real castle, for our friends only occupied the more modern portion of it. All the rest was in ruins, or nearly so.

It was within sound of the roar of a cataract, which could be heard ever and aye in drowsy monotony, except on stormy nights, when the wild wind, sweeping through the tall dark pine trees that grew on a beetling cliff-top behind the ruin, quite drowned even the voice of the linn.

It was a rare old house and ruin for cats and children to play about; for there was not only quite a jungle of cover for birds of every sort, but the ivy itself that covered some of the sturdy grey walls gave berth and bield to more than one brown owl.

It was perhaps the noise made by the owls that gave rise to the notion, ripe enough among the peasantry, that the old Castle was haunted.

Lizzie and her brother both believed in this ghost.
They made themselves believe, in fact, because it was
romantic so to do.

There were fine old-fashioned walled-in gardens and
lawns to play in besides, so that on the whole it was a kind
of ideal place.

There was one peculiarity about the lawn that I should
tell you of. The Colonel would not have it kept closely
shaven. He loved to see the daisies growing thereon, and
many a pink, crimson, or yellow nodding wild flower as
well.

So all the summer long it was beautiful, and even in
autumn too.

Lizzie and Tom were such gentle children, that none of
the creatures of nature which visited the lawn, seemed to
be one whit afraid of them. In fact, they—the children—
were part and parcel of all that was beautiful in nature
around them.

The mavises sang to them nearly all the year through,
sometimes even in snow time. So did cock-robin, because
he was always fed, even in summer. Lizzie and Tom
knew where his nest was in a bank of wild roses, and
robin appeared rather pleased than otherwise to have
them come quietly round and take a peep at his yellow-
throated gaping gorblings of youngsters.

"It takes me all my time," cock robin told Lizzie, "and
all my wife's time too, to feed them. Oh, they do eat and
eat and eat to be sure. It is just stuff, stuff, stuff all day
long; one beetle down the other come on, so that I haven't
time to sing a song to you. But wait till winter comes,
and the youngsters are up and away, and won't I just
sing!"

There was a saucy rascal of a blackbird that used to run about on the lawn gathering food, quite close to the children. When Shireen, Tabby, and the rest were there the blackbird used to come even closer, in order that he might nod his head and scold the cats.

But Dick would cry "Eh? Eh? What d'ye say? What is it? You r—r—rascal!" and sometimes even fly down to offer him battle.

There was no song more sweet in the summer evenings however, than blackie's.

The owl kept his song till midnight, and a very dreary one it was!

But strangely enough, some may think it, yet it is nevertheless most true, wild pigeons built their nests in the pine trees, close to the wall in which the owls had theirs. These pigeons knew, though gamekeepers don't, that these owls lived on young rats and mice and not upon birds.

Squirrels used to run about the lawn with their long brown beautiful tails behind them, early in the morning; and they built in trees also.

Then there was a white-breasted weasel, that would often come quite close up to Lizzie and Tom, and stand on one end to look at what they were doing.

On this particular year, autumn lingered long on the hills and forests and fields all around the children's beautiful home. It was, Uncle Ben said, a real Indian summer, so soft and warm and mellow, that neither he nor the Colonel ever cared to be much indoors.

"Well,"—said Warlock, one afternoon out on the Colonel's lawn, while Lizzie and Tom sat at some distance making a garland of gowans for the dogs' necks, and the old sailor and soldier sat in their straw chairs, peacefully smoking and yarning—"Well, Shireen, although I have never been to sea myself, considering that the land and the lovely hills and woods are good enough for me, I dearly like to hear about it, so just heave round with your yarn, as Uncle Ben yonder says."

"Yes, with pleasure," said Shireen.   "Let me see though, where did I leave off?"

"Why you left yourself sitting on the bulwark of the old *Venom*, catching flying fish."

Oh, yes, so I did, Warlock.   My memory is just getting a little fickle now, while yours is supple and green.   Well, the voyage south was continued, slowly though, because we kept in towards the green-wooded coast, you know, in order to hunt for slave ships.   And several times Tom Brandy and I had to be blown out of the gun with a fuze before the men could load it.   I always knew what was going to happen when this took place, and ran aft right speedily and got down below to my master's bed ; because do what I might, I could never reconcile myself to the noise of those terrible guns.

Master I could see, much to my joy, was getting better and stronger every day.   But he often spoke to me about my mistress Beebee, and always said that he would, at all risks, prevent her from being sold to the Shah.

One day he went so far as to say, "Dear pussy Shireen, your mistress is much too good and too beautiful for a fellow like the Shah.   Let him be content with the slaves he has.   He is only a savage himself, at the best, and rather than he should have your sweet mistress, I will go back to Persia and carry her away."

My life on board the *Venom* was now a most happy and

pleasant one ; but often and often, Warlock, I dreamt that
I was back again in the land of the lion and the sun, in
beautiful Persia, and that I was sitting as of old in the
turret balcony, with my darling mistress. Then I would
awake and find myself far away on the dark blue sea.

No, I should not say dark blue sea, because the Indian
Ocean is more lovely far than turquoisine.

Tom Brandy and I would sit for hours on the bulwarks,
which I used to call a fence, looking at the sea. The
flying-fish knew far better than to come on board the
vessel during the day, but there always was something or
other to be seen in the ocean. At times, especially on
calm days, it would be a shoal of silvery whitebait. And
such a shoal! Oh, Tabby, it would have made your
mouth water to look upon it. We could see first far
ahead of us, a dark patch upon the bright blue water, and
when we came nearer, that part of the sea would be all
a-quiver, as if it were raining hard there and nowhere else.
But soon the shoal opened out in all its beauty of silvery
life and loveliness. I'm not a poet, only a Persian cat,
else I could describe it better

"Oh, rats !" cried Warlock, "never mind the poetry."

Another sight we used to see would be a shoal of
dolphins.

"Chasing the whitebait, I suppose ?" This from Warlock.

"I didn't say so, Warlock."

But very prettily they used to come along on the top of
the water They would be so far away at first that they
looked like tiny black ticks on the horizon, but soon they
were near enough to us, and we saw that they were
monsters. Oh, a hundred times as large as you, Warlock,

or all of us put together. They came up head first, and
went down head first, just skylarking and playing and
skipping like lambs on the leas. And the water all
around them was lashed into foam. Wasn't I afraid, did
you ask me, Vee-Vee? No, not a bit, because Tom told
me they were as harmless as cows

But, my children, there were creatures in that deep sea
of turquoisine that were very far indeed from being harmless. These were the sharks.

There were always one or two down there that the
doctor fed. They used to know the doctor, and floated
alongside the ship, while he threw down pieces of fat to
them, and sometimes a ham bone.

The doctor said those tigers of the ocean used to
swallow whatever was thrown overboard, even if it were
only an empty medicine bottle.

Sometimes they looked very lovingly at the doctor, and
this officer would tell me they were asking him to throw
over a cat for them to swallow. They said they had never
eaten cat, but felt sure that it must taste very nice indeed.

But little did we think that one day we would be in
danger of our lives from those awful monsters.

Only it wasn't by day, but by night, and a clear and
beautiful night it was too, with the moon shining as
brightly almost as it used to shine over the woods around
my Persian home.

Tom and I had been sitting on the bulwarks as usual,
expecting a flying fish to come on board. But they could
see us too distinctly, so they kept away.

There was very little wind that night, just enough to
fill the sails, and carry us along about five knots an
hour.

It was a few minutes past midnight, and the watch had been changed, and stillness reigned everywhere. I think I must have fallen asleep and been dreaming, for I started in fright when one bell was struck loudly and clearly.

I started so that I missed my balance, and fell with a plash into the sea. Next moment Tom Brandy uttered a plaintive howl and dashed in after me. I am sure that the poor fellow had no idea of trying to save my life, he only wished to share my fate.

I heard a shout just after Tom came down. For a man in the watch, hearing the plash in the water, immediately concluded that someone had fallen in, and raised the alarm.

"Man overboard! Away, lifeboat's crew!"

The shout was taken up and repeated fore and aft, down below and on deck as well.

Then something came rushing down into the sea from the stern of the ship, and fell into the water with a strange hollow ring.

The officer of the watch had let go the lifebuoy, but so quickly that he had forgotten to light it. His neglect to do so probably saved our lives.

The lifebuoy is made of two empty copper balls, with an arm of wood between. From this rises a short mast, on the top of which a beacon burns. Now had this been lit, Tom and I would have burned our paws when we scrambled up the little mast.

I never knew I could swim till then, but I can assure you, Warlock, it didn't take Tom Brandy and I long to reach that lifebuoy, and there we clung till the boat came.

It was not long, perhaps, till the boat did arrive, but to me it seemed like a hundred years, for the sea all around us appeared to be alive with awful sharks. Tom told me afterwards my eyes must have multiplied their numbers, and that there were only just the doctor's two tame ones.

Well, Warlock, tame or not tame, they wanted to tear Tom and me to pieces, and were terribly disappointed when the men took us on board and the boat went rushing back to the *Venom* with us rescued pussies.

When the captain heard of what he called the gallant rescue, he ordered the mainbrace to be spliced, and so the men all had a glass of grog for saving our lives.

But next day the seaman who had struck the bell which so startled me, informed the boatswain that he was positive both cats did not fall off the bulwarks, but that I only had missed my hold and tumbled into the sea. He looked quickly towards the bows he said, and for a second or two saw Tom Brandy there safe enough. Then he heard his cry, and saw him deliberately spring into the sea after me.

The boatswain told all this to the men and also to the officers, and after that Tom became indeed a hero on board the ship. My master spoke of presenting him with a handsome collar of solid silver. The armourer said if my master Edgar would let him have the silver, he would very soon make it and engrave it also; he received a large silver spoon, and so heartily did he work, that in less than a week Tom was wearing his collar.

But, children, continued Shireen thoughtfully, although Tom Brandy looked somewhat dignified in his silver collar, it is rather a risky ornament for a pussy to wear. For a cat friend of mine in the country being presented with a lovely morocco leather collar by his own mistress, who thought a great deal of him, disappeared soon after

THE SEA AROUND WAS ALIVE WITH SHARKS.

in the most mysterious way. A whole week passed by and poor Clytie didn't appear. Then one day a boy rang the door bell, and asked to see Clytie's mistress. He thought he had found the missing cat he said.

" Where, my dear boy, where?" cried Mrs. L——

" Up in a tree, far down in the wood, ma'am."

" And why didn't you bring him? I'll go with you, and we must get him, and I will pay you well."

" Can you climb trees?" she added.

" Like a squirrel," he said boldly.

The tree was soon found, and up swarmed the boy.

" It is Clytie right enough!" he shouted down; "but she's been and gone and hung herself."

" Oh, poor pussy! Is she dead?"

By this time the lad was coming down the tree with pussy under his jacket.

" Never a dead is she, ma'am, but awfully thin."

She was indeed thin, and a miserable time she must have spent. A branch of the tree had got caught in the collar, and there the poor cat was hung up by the neck, and but for the boy, who perhaps had been birds'-nesting, she would have been slowly starved to death.

That's the worst of a dandy collar. But nothing ever happened to Tom Brandy on board the ship.

Well, in due course the *Venom* arrived safely in port, and was paid off. And I assure you, dear children, the day I parted from Tom Brandy I was very sorry indeed. But, you see, he wasn't my master's cat, and so couldn't go with us.

Indeed Captain Beecroft had taken a real fancy for Tom, and being like many sailors, just a little super-stitious, he thought that if he parted with pussy, all his good luck would go also, so he determined to stick to him.

Arrived on shore, we, that is my dear master and I, went to Yorkshire to live for a time with an aunt of his, about the only relative he had alive.

Mrs. Clifford was an exceedingly nice old lady, and very fond of cats, as every nice old lady is, you know, Warlock. She took quite a fancy to me at once, and I had the run of the house and gardens, and a fine old-fashioned place it was. There were several other cats here and dogs too, but we lived like a happy family just as we all do here.

"Now, pussy Shireen," said master to me one evening, "I don't know what I shall do. I think more and more about your beautiful mistress that the Shah is going to claim, every day of my life; and I think, too, of the vow I made to protect her from the terrible fate that awaits her. But oh, pussy, I'm almost in a fix, for I must tell aunt about Beebee, and, very nice though she is, I do not know how she may take it; I am entirely dependent upon her, and what is more, I am her heir."

"But tell her I must, Shireen, even if she cuts me off with a shilling. I still have my sword, you know, pussy."

I rubbed my head against his hand, and sang loud and long.

He understood me, and took me up in his arms and kissed me on the head.

"Yes, Shireen," he said, "I still have you, and we shall never part, I do assure you, unless I am slain in battle, and even then you will be by my side."

Then he started to his feet.

"Come, Shireen," he said bravely, "the more I think

about it, the worse it will be. I will go and seek my aunt now in her own room, and tell her all about it."

I trotted along the passage with him, and soon we came to Mrs. Clifford's door.

"Come in," she cried. "Come in, Edgar," for she knew it was his knock.

"Sit down, my child, by my chair."

So Edgar took a low stool by her knee just as he used to do when a boy, and the kindly white-haired lady passed her hand through his hair.

"Just like old times, isn't it, Edgar?"

"Yes, auntie; but I have come to speak to you about Shireen."

"About your beautiful pussy?"

"Yes. Look, auntie."

Edgar, as he spoke, took me up and exposed my gum.

"Do you see that brilliant red flashing little spot, aunt?"

"Yes, my dear boy. Let me get my glasses. Why, I declare, Edgar, it is a brilliant, a ruby, and though small, it looks like a priceless gem."

"And so it is; and the person who had it put there is a still more priceless gem to me."

"I don't understand you, Edgar; you always were a strange child."

"Well, shall I tell you the story of the ruby?"

Mrs. Clifford folded her mittened hands in her lap, and looked, or tried to look, resigned.

"I think," she said, "I know what is coming. You have been out in Persia, and you have fallen in love with some designing minx of a Persian girl, and she gave you that Persian cat—and—and—and—" here the old lady began

K

to tap with her foot against the footstool—"oh, that my brother's boy should have fallen in love with a blacka· moor!"

Edgar at this moment pulled out a case from his pocket, and opening it by means of touching a spring, held out before his auntie's astonished gaze a charmingly-executed miniature portrait of my sweet mistress.

" Is that a blackamoor, auntie?" he said.

"This lovely child! Is this——" she spoke no more for a time.

But my master knew he had gained a point, so he com- menced to tell Beebee's story and mine, from the very beginning to the end, and I assure you, children, when he finished, the tears were silently falling down the furrowed cheeks of the dear white-haired lady

"Oh, the inhuman monster of a father of the dear girl!" she said, as if speaking to herself.

Then she turned to my master and held out her hand.

"Dear boy," she said, " I am your friend, and if ever Beebee comes to this country, I will try to be a friend and a mother to her."

Then Edgar got up. He kissed the lady's white hair, then walked straight away out of the room, struggling hard to restrain the tears that filled his eyes

They were tears of joy though.

CHAPTER XIV.

UST a few weeks after this, and while reading a letter at breakfast, my master's face flushed with joy.

There was nobody in the room but me, for the old lady did not come down to breakfast very early.

" Why, pussy Shireen, what do you think ? " he cried.

Of course, I couldn't tell what the matter might be.

" My regiment—the 78th Highlanders—has been ordered to Persia, to give the Persians a drubbing for insolence to our Government, and if I am well enough I must join forthwith. Hurrah! Of course I'm well enough.

" There will be many regiments there as well as ours, but oh, Shireen! won't it be joyful, and you must come too, pussy. It may seem strange for the captain of a gallant regiment to have a cat as a pet, but what care I ? Many a brave soldier has loved his pussy, so you come along with me, and I'll chance it.

" Now," he added, " I'll just write a letter to the War Office, saying that I am well, and burning to join my regiment, then I'll go down the hill and post it before auntie is up. That will settle it."

Well, of course, children, Mrs. Clifford was very sorry to lose her dear Edgar, as she called him, so soon again; but she was a brave old lady, and though she cried a little, she gave him a blessing and bade him go.

"Duty must be obeyed, Edgar," she said, "even though hearts should break. Go, my boy, your country calls you."

I don't think, children, there was a much happier cat than pussy Shireen on the day my master left Waterloo Station for Portsmouth, to take passage for Bombay in a ship of war, especially when the brave soldier told me that this ship was to be commanded by Captain Beecroft himself. Indeed, hearing that we were going to India to join our regiment for service in Persia, Captain Beecroft had written to us, offering us a passage, and saying he would be very glad indeed to have master once more on board his vessel. And, he added, as master knew none of the officers in the ward-room, he would be happy to have him as a guest in his own apartments.

We had not gone straight to London, I may tell you, Warlock, from Yorkshire. We had a run over to Dublin first to see a friend, and on board the steamer I astonished everybody by my perfect coolness. I even ran right up the rigging into the foretop, and had a look around me, and the sailors all declared I was a ship's cat born and bred.

Well, we had arrived at our hotel in the evening. I may tell you that it stood in one of the principal streets, and right in the middle of it, so that anyone going out by a back window and across the tiles, would have to go a long way round to get to the front door again.

Of course, Warlock, no human being would have dreamt of going out at a back window and along the tiles, and no dog either. But it is precisely what I did when master shut me in the room, and locked me in for safety till he should post a letter.

When he returned, behold! no Shireen was there, and he called me from the window in vain.

The truth is, I had never been to Ireland before, and wanted to see what the Irish cats were like ; so I determined to spend a night on the tiles and go home with the milk in the morning.

I can't say, however, that I thoroughly enjoyed myself. I found the Dublin cats a rather disreputable gang. They serenaded nervous old gentlemen, and had water and brushes and lumps of coal and the boot-jack thrown at them ; they scratched up beds of choice flowers, and they broke into pigeon-lofts, and dove-cots, and killed and ate the pigeons. Moreover, they boasted of all these exploits as if they had been the greatest fun in the world. So, on the whole, I was somewhat disgusted. However, it opened up a new phase of life before me, and so I gained some experience.

But, children, you must not suppose that I, a silken-coated Persian and a brave soldier's cat, kept with this gang all night. I did not, but retired into a garden arbour early in the evening to have a quiet talk with a lady cat who, it was evident from her voice and manners, had seen better days.

She was a very pretty half-bred Angora, or rather, I should say, she had been pretty once upon a time, but at present her face was thin and worn, her eyes looked world-weary, and her coat hung around her in mats and tatters.

"And so," she said, after we had settled down face to face, "and so you have been far travelled, and come all the way from across the seas?"

"Yes," I answered, "and I am going all the way back again. The fact is, I have no real home, except where master is, and I do not care where that may be, whether on the lonesome moorland, amidst the city's bustle, din, and strife, or far away upon the lone blue sea, I say, that if he be with me I am at home."

"Ah!" sighed the poor waif in front of me. "I wish I had a kind master or mistress, if so you wouldn't find me here to-night. Why, I haven't even a name now, though they used to call me Zulina."

"A pretty name," I said; "but tell me, Zulina, how did so ladylike-looking and evidently amiable a pussy as you become a nomad and a wanderer?"

"Oh, don't call me amiable," she answered: "indeed, I am not. All my amiability, and even love, for the human race, has been crushed out of me. Well, once I had a home in the outskirts of this very city, and many home-ties too. It was a pretty house, with gardens all around it, and custom and long residence thereat had much endeared me to it. I knew every hole and corner of it. Knew every mouse-run, the cupboards, and the cosy nooks where I could have a quiet snooze when I needed such refreshment, and the places in which I could hide when hiding became an absolute necessity. I was acquainted with the manner of egress and ingress, so that I felt free and untrammelled, and I was familiar with every sound so that my rest was never disturbed by night, nor my nerves jarred by day.

"And out of doors too, Shireen, everything about the

SHIREEN AND ZULINA.

dear old place was familiar to me ; the trees on which the sparrows perched, the field where I often found an egg, the meadow where the wild rabbits played, and the paths by which I could reach it in safety.

" But I was taken away from this home by a mistress who used to profess such love for me, and removed to a town more than twenty miles from Dublin. My new home too, was right in the centre of the town, and everything about it looked strange and foreign to me. But so long as I felt sure my mistress loved me, I did not care, so I began to learn the place by heart, as it were, and all the outs and ins of it.

" But lo! what was my astonishment to hear my mistress say one day :

" ' I don't think we can put up with that cat now in this new house. I think we had better give a boy sixpence to drown it to-morrow morning.'

" That night I left the house, and the ungrateful mistress I had loved so well and dearly. I left the house, and the town too, and wandered on and on nearly all night, and at early dawn I was back again at my dear-loved home.

" I had forgotten there were strangers there now. And they treated me as a stray cat, and drummed me out when I dared to put my nose over the threshold.

" What could I do, Shireen ? I could not endure the pangs of hunger, and though I hung about the garden of my old home for days, and made many a plaintive but useless appeal to the new-comers, I was forced at last to cast aside the mantle of virtue and become a thief. Yes, I even broke into the new people's pigeon-loft and stole a bird. Then I took to this evil existence, and since then, alas! I have never been inside a human habitation except to steal."

"Well, Zulina, it is very sad," I said; "but I think you should try to reform even yet, and some kind lady might take pity on you."

"No, no, no," sighed Zulina, "I am but a homeless waif and stray, and my fate, I fear, will be to die in the street, or be torn to pieces by dogs."

"I'm going to hope for better things for you, Zulina," I insisted. "But good-bye. Yonder is the grey dawn stealing up into the sky, and I think I hear the milkman's cry in a distant street. I must try to find my master's hotel. Good-bye."

It was a long distance round, but my instinct was unerring, and finally I found myself trotting up the correct street, and soon after sitting in the area doorway.

Down came the milkman with his rattling cans, and in a minute or two, Biddy, with her hair in papers, and looking very sleepy, opened the door.

While Biddy and the milkman were interchanging a few courtesies, I slipped quietly into the house and made my way as fast as I could upstairs to the second floor.

I soon spied my master's boots, and mewed at the door.

It was opened in a moment, and in I popped, purring as loudly as I knew how to.

"Oh! pussy, pussy," he cried, as he picked me up, "I thought I would never see you more, and I was quite disconsolate. You went out by the back and over the tiles, and now you've come in at the front; how did you find your way round?

"It is instinct, instinct, I suppose," he added. "He who guides the great fur seals back through the stormy seas, through hundreds of miles of darkness and mist to their far northern islands in June, He guided you.

"'Reason raise o'er instinct if we can,
In this 'tis God directs, in that 'tis man.'"

＊

Well, Warlock, we left Dublin, and at last found ourselves at Waterloo Station.

The train was in, and I was in also. I was in a basket, and I didn't half like it.

I heard my master say to a railway porter, "Take charge of that basket for a few minutes, porter, till I go and buy some newspapers."

Five minutes after this, when Edgar returned, he met that railway porter, and he was looking very disconsolate indeed.

His hands were bleeding, and he carried an empty basket.

"Oh! sir," he cried, "your cat has gone. The basket was not securely fastened, and as soon as you left she wriggled out."

"But why, man, didn't you stick to her?" cried master.

"I tried to all I could, I do assure you, sir; but she bit me and tore my hands, then jumped down and disappeared in the crowd."

"Well, come along and take my things out of the compartment where we put them, for I shan't go by this train."

"I'm so sorry, sir. But she's only a cat, sir. You could get another."

"Do as you're told, porter, please," said my master imperiously.

Without another word the porter followed him to the first-class compartment, and there they found me cosily snuggled up among the rugs.*

Master was delighted, and gave the porter half-a-sovereign to heal his wounded dignity, and his still more wounded fingers.

My children, I travelled many and many a thousand miles with master after that both by sea and by land, but never again did he insult my *amour propre* by putting me in a creel.

At this moment Lizzie and Tom joined the group of old friends on the lawn. Tom threw himself down on the grass, and began to twine the garland of gowans he had been making around the neck of Vee-Vee, the Pomeranian dog.

Vee-Vee was Tom's favourite, and never a night would the boy go to bed without him.

No, Vee-Vee did not sleep *in* the bed, but on a couch in the same cosy little room. He was exceedingly fond of the boy, a proof that love begets love, and of course the doggie would be always first awake in the morning, but he would not stir until Tommy did. As soon, however, as the little lad sighed, his first waking sigh, Vee-Vee jumped joyfully up on the bed, and his delight was simply wonderful.

---

* This incident occurred just as described, the *dramatis personæ* being the author and his own far-travelled cat Muffie II.

How nice to be awakened thus by one who loves you, even if it be but a dog.

Vee-Vee was quite as rapturous in the welcome with which he used to greet Tommy's home-coming, if he happened to be away all day.

During the lad's absence the dog would refuse all food, and simply lie in the hall with eyes open and ears erect until he heard his little master's voice or footstep; then he would spring up quite beside himself with joy, his bark having a kind of half hysterical ring in it, as if tears were hindering its clearer utterance.

Vee-Vee now seemed rejoiced to get the garland of gowans. It was a mark of favour on the part of Tommy that he acknowledged by licking his hands and cheek.

Meanwhile Lizzie had brought out a rug to place on the grass, that she might sit thereon, and so save herself from the damp.

As she was spreading it on the green sward something tumbled out.

That something was Chammy.

"Oh, Chammy, Chammy!" cried Lizzie delighted, "we thought you were dead. Where *will* you hide next?"

But Chammy gathered himself slowly up and crawled away, one leg at a time, to look for a fly.

CHAPTER XV.

OBODY had ever been heard to call Cracker a pretty dog or a bonnie dog. He was sturdy and strong, and nearly, if not quite, as large as a Collie. His legs were as straight as darts, and as strong as the sapling pine tree. Then his coat—ah! well, there is no way of describing that with pen and ink or in print either. It was rough though not shaggy, and every hair was as hard apparently as pin-wire.

In the matter of coats, in fact, Nature had, while dressing Cracker, adhered to the useful rather than the ornamental. He had apparently come in the afternoon for his coat, and nearly all the other dogs had been before him. Collie had been fitted with his flowing toga, the Poodle with his cords and tassels, the Yorkshire terrier with his doublet of silk, and many others with coats as soft and smooth as that of a carriage horse, and poor Cracker, the Airdale terrier, had almost been forgotten.

"Your coat, Cracker?" Nature had said. "Oh, certainly. I'm really afraid, however, that you have come rather late in the day to be dressed with anything like elegance."

"Oh!" Cracker had put in, "I ain't a bit particular. Anything 'll do for Cracker, so as it is thick enough to keep out a shower with a shake."

So Nature had simply gathered up the sweepings of the shop, the cabbage and clippings, so to speak, and mixed them all up into a kind of shoddy, and dabbed Cracker all over with that, going in, however, for a few finishing touches of gold about the muzzle, the chest, and legs.

And good honest Cracker had given himself a shake, and said, "This'll do famous," then trotted off to do his duty and his work, which, to his credit be it said, every dog of this breed knows well how to get through.

Well, one sunshiny day, when the old friends, including even Chammy, who was lying in the limb of a dwarf holly, were assembled on Uncle Ben's lawn, Ben himself and the Colonel blowing clouds in their straw chairs, and Lizzie lying with a book in Ben's hammock, who should come through the gateway but towsy Cracker himself.

He was a brave dog this, and just as modest as brave, for the two good qualities always go hand-in-hand. So he advanced in a bashful, hesitating kind of way, as if he felt he ought to apologise for his presence on the lawn at all, but didn't know exactly how to begin. He was smiling too, a very broad smile that seemed to extend half way down both sides.

Vee-Vee and Warlock jumped up at once growling and barking, and ready to defend the family circle with their lives if there was any occasion, but seeing it was only Cracker, they ran to meet him, and give him a hearty welcome.

Then Cracker advanced, shaking his droll old stump of

a tail, and Shireen herself arose and rubbed her back against his legs.

"No," she said, "you certainly don't intrude, Cracker, and we only wish you would come oftener than you do."

"Well, seeing as that's the case," said Cracker, "I'll make one this afternoon at your little garden party. But I'm not much used to refined society, I bet you. More at home in a stable than in a drawing-room; the riverside and moor or the forest is more in old Cracker's way than fountain, lawn, and shrubbery. But, la! Shireen, whatever is that lying along that branch? It isn't a big snail and it ain't a large slug, sometimes grey and sometimes green. Well, of all the ugly——"

"It's a friend of ours," said Shireen, interrupting Cracker, "and, I assure you, Chammy won't hurt anything or anybody except the flies and mealworms."

"Well, well," said Cracker, "wonders 'ill never cease, but if I had met a beast like that in the woods, I'd have bolted quick, you bet, and never turned tail till safe in my kennel again."

"And now, Mother Shireen, let us have some more of your story," said Vee-Vee.

"Ah! yes," said Tabby; "but what a pity Cracker didn't hear the first part."

Well, said Shireen, we arrived at Portsmouth, I and my master as safe as anything, and after dinner proceeded on board.

The *Hydra* was the name of the war-ship on which we were to sail for India's distant shore. She was a fine craft of the kind human beings call a corvette. I was not long in perceiving that she carried many long black guns, but was glad to learn soon after my arrival, that as we were going to make a very quick passage out to Bombay, these awful guns would hardly ever be fired.

The *Hydra* was much larger than the old *Venom*, had fine open decks, and tall, raking masts, with a low, wide funnel of jet, up which went the crimson copper steampipe. Her decks were as white as ivory, and I could see my face in the polished woodwork, to say nothing of the brass that shone like gold.

I trotted along by my master's side towards the quarter-deck.

Captain Beecroft in uniform, and looking young and happy, came forward with a smile to bid us welcome.

" So you haven't parted with your beautiful cat?" said the captain, as we walked to the companion.

" No, Beecroft, nothing, I hope, will ever part me from her."

" I wonder," said Beecroft, "if she'll remember her old pal, the hero, Tom Brandy."

" What? Have you still got Tom?"

" Yes. It isn't likely I'd sail without black Tom. That would be to throw away my luck, you know, and I'd never become an Admiral."

" Ha, ha, ha!" laughed master; "but how superstitious sailors are!"

" And some soldiers too, ain't they? Ha, ha!"

Then both laughed, and Beecroft led the way to his quarters, a sentry at the door saluting as we passed by.

I declare to you, children, when I saw honest Tom Brandy lying there on a skin rug in front of the stove— for it was almost winter now, and very cold—you could have knocked me down with a sledge hammer.

L.

I felt all over in a whirl with joy, and for a moment I didn't know whether my top or my toes were uppermost.

Tom jumped up with a fond cry, and ran to meet me, and the two of us ran round and round the table in order to allay our feelings, like a pair of three-month-old kittens.

But we both settled down on the skin in a few minutes, and commenced singing a duet together, to the accompaniment of a coffee-urn that simmered above the stove.

"Just like old times, isn't it, soldier?" said Beecroft, looking down at me and Tom.

"Just like old times, sailor," said master.

Then the two shook hands once more.

And down they sat to talk and smoke.

The ship sailed in a day or two, heading away down channel on a beam wind. Tom told me it was a beam wind, else I wouldn't have known, for it was just the same colour as any other wind. Tom also told me we were under close-reefed topsails and storm jib, and that if it came on to blow a bit more, we should be scudding under bare poles.

I said, "Oh, indeed!" But I didn't know in the least what Tom meant.

You will observe, children, that Tom was dreadfully learned and nautical.

He was looking far more respectable and beautiful than when I saw him last. He had a new coat of jetty black, and there wasn't a single burnt hole in it. He was rounder in the face, too, and more brilliant in eye.

When I remarked upon these improvements.

"Oh," he said, "it is like this, Shireen, I have been living in the bosom of the Captain's own family on shore, and on the fat of the land, as you might say.

"I've turned over a new leaf too," he added, looking pensively at the blazing, caking coal, and swaying to and fro with the motion of the ship. "When I came on board the old *Venom* I wasn't what you might have called strictly honest. I would have laid hands on a herring at any time; and I once tried to eat the cook's canary, and was beautifully basted in consequence. But I've seen the error of my ways, and now that I am the Captain's cat, I consider it is more honourable to beg than to steal. But my eyes, Shireen, how beautiful you're looking! And to think I've got you back again. Won't we have some jolly larks, and won't we catch some flying fish. A few, eh? But mind you, Shireen, no going to sleep on the bulwarks and tumbling into the sea, this cruise."

"Oh, it makes me shudder to think of that wild adventure, Tom," I said.

"Yes, those sharks pretty nearly had us, hadn't they, Shireen? If they hadn't set to quarrelling among themselves as to which would have the white cat and which the black, they'd have eaten us both."

"Heigho!" I sighed, and looked at Tom.

"Heigho!" sighed Tom, and looked at me.

Then we went on with the duet.

*　　　　*　　*　　　　*　　*

The weather soon grew so warm and balmy, and

beautiful, that there was no longer any need for a fire in the stove, and the captain's steward took away the skin, and put down a clean straw mat, and covered the sofa with coolest white and blue chintz, and the ports were carried open all day long, so that we could feel the breeze, and see the dark rippling ocean rushing past us, all bespangled with splashes of sunshine.

I was of course quite an old sailor, though I couldn't speak nautical like Tom, and I enjoyed this cruise even more than the last.

So I ought to. Was not every day taking me nearer and nearer to my dear little mistress Beebee? And the shorter the time, the more I seemed to love her.

"Instead of going away from home," said dear master to me one day in the cabin, "I seem to be going to my home, and going to happiness. Oh, I do hope, Shireen, that something will turn up for our good. The fortunes of war are so changeable, you know, Shireen, and we may see Beebee, may be able even to save her from her fate; but——alas! we may not."

We rounded the Cape in wild weather. The waves were mountains high, children; thunder roared and shook the ship, and lightning flash, quickly following flash, played around us, till all the ocean looked like a vast sea of fire. I was almost as much afraid of the thunder as I had been of the great guns on board the saucy *Venom.*

But soon we got out of this region of storms, and went north and away, the weather getting warmer day after day.

We were soon in the delightful regions of the flying fish; but I took great care not to fall asleep again on the bulwarks.

Everything looked the same in this great turquoisine sea; the bonitoes, the flying fish, the dancing, cooing dolphins, and even those terrible sly-eyed tigers of the sea —the sharks.

On and on and north and north we went. Sometimes we passed a green island, that seemed to hang in the air, rather than float on the ocean; and sometimes the surface of the water was patched here and there with glass-green or pearl-grey, and I knew, or rather Tom told me, that we were sailing over shoals, and at night extra look-outs had to be set, lest we should strike the coral rocks, and the ship break up, when we should all be drowned, and I should never see my mistress more.

It was what they call the cool season when we reached Bombay at last. But such a bustling, busy scene, never did I see before in all my life!

It was baggage and stores here, there, and everywhere, and soldiers all about, and boats skimming the water in every direction; and drums beating, bugles blowing, and great Highland bagpipes screaming, till I declare to you, children, it made me quite dizzy. The worst of it was, that for some days now I didn't see so much of my master, though you may be sure I took good care to be at his side whenever I could.

I was sorry when the time came to part with Tom again, but we plighted our troth, and promised never to forget the happy cruise in the *Hydra*.

When it was all over and we were once more at sea, *en route* for the Persian Gulf, I gave a great sigh of relief. But I did feel a little lonely without Tom Brandy, and kept all the more closely to my master in consequence.

I was now to become a soldier's cat in downright earnest, and know something about the horrors of war.

Shireen paused for a moment.

"Cracker," she said, "do you like the story?"

"It's a beauty," said Cracker, "and I'll like it still better when the fighting commences and the fur begins to fly."

CHAPTER XVI.

THE FIGHT WAS HAND TO HAND AND HORRIBLE!

ELL, Cracker, my dear friend, the fighting did begin in earnest, and soon too after we landed, though I'm sure I was very much puzzled indeed, and tried in vain to make out what it all meant.

How I wished that Tom had been there to help me, for I think Tom knew nearly everything worth knowing.

For the first time now I saw my master in full fighting array. He called his fine clothes his war-paint, and he drew a huge long knife out of a holder, and showed me how sharp it was, and said he was going to do and die in his country's cause.

I wasn't quite sure what doing and dying in a country's cause was. But from the very commencement I knew that those soldier-men made a terrible din.

My master, in his gallant uniform and long sharp knife, belonged to the gay Highlanders, and they were the first sent on shore, and marched about in line and wheeled and tacked to the sound of the skirling bagpipes, with no other idea, I thought, than just to show off their fine clothes.

War, I began to think, must be very nice indeed.

Ah! but Cracker, the fur hadn't begun to fly yet.

Well, master's servant was a very tall fighting-man of the Highlanders, whom his comrades called Jock McNab.

"McNab," said my master one day.

The red-faced, big pleasant man saluted

"What's your wull?" said Jock McNab

"Shireen knows you well by this time."

"Ah! 'deed she does," said Jock, "and lo'es me too."

"Well, Mac, we've both got to look after her. Do you think when we get into grips with the enemy, that Shireen would sit on top of your knapsack?"

"Weel," said Jock, "if you'll gie me leave, sir, I'll soon drill her to that."

So Jock took me in hand that very evening after we reached camp, and began to teach me what he called "knapsack drill."

It was very simple. I was put on top of the knapsack and Jock fixed the bayonet on his gun and commenced plunging about up and down, and high and low, as if in front of the enemy. But I set my nails firmly into the knapsack and nothing could shake me off.

"That'll do fine for a beginning," said Jock.

There were British soldiers in the entrenched camp before Bushire, when we landed there, and marched to it, and right hearty welcome they made us.

The camp was in the middle of a vast plain, on which grew here and there some clumps of palm trees, and here and there a ruin stood. To our left was the blue sea, with the far-off shipping. Some distance in front of us was the walled town itself, built upon a long spit of land, and washed nearly all round by the sea. Far away behind the town were the lofty mountains, their snowy heads rising high into the azure sky.

" Poetry again !" said Warlock.

" A spice of poesy," said Shireen grandly, "sometimes adds attraction to a scene. Don't you think so, Cracker ? "

" Well, Shireen, to tell you the truth I can't say I understand it like. My mother used to say to me ' Cracker,' she said, ' in your journey through this vale of tears, always make a better use of your teeth than your tongue.' "

" Very good," said Warlock. " Your mother must have been a brick, Cracker."

" A brick, Warlock. What a funny idea ! No, no, my mother was a Bingley terrier. But go on, Shireen, when did the fur begin to fly ? "

Not yet a bit, Cracker. Well, at night, I found my way to master's tent, and was glad to snuggle up in his arms, for though the days were warm the nights were bitterly cold.

Just before I fell asleep, Jock McNab came to the tent.

" I'm sayin', sir," he said.

" Yes, Mac, what is it ? "

" Is Shireen wi' you ? "

" That she is. Thank you, McNab, for being so mindful."

" That's a' richt then," said Jock. " Good-nicht."

And away the faithful fellow went.

Now although we were lying in camp here before Bushire, we weren't going to attack this town. Indeed, the people seemed very glad to see us, and sold us all kinds of nice things. So our brave General Outram soon got ready to make a terrible attack upon an entrenched camp of the Persians, fifty miles distant, and we had to walk all the way.

What a beautiful sight it was, I thought, to see all those brave soldiers in lines and lines, outside the camp; horses, Highlanders, and even fighting sailors and artillerymen. Of course you won't understand all I am saying, Cracker, but I am a soldier's cat, you know, and cannot help feeling a little martial ardour when I think of that splendid campaign.

Well, off we marched at last, my master at the head of his company, and I, perched on Jock McNab's knapsack, but keeping master in my eye all the time.

What a long weary, dreary march that was to Char Kota!

"Eh? Eh? What is it?" said the starling. "What d'ye say?"

"I said Char Kota, Dick, but I'm not going to use any hard names if I can help it, you may be sure."

Well, continued Shireen, the village I mentioned is twenty-six miles from the shore, but after a long halt we fell in again, and it was ten o'clock at night before we got to the place where we were to rest till morning.

Oh, how tired and weary the poor fellows were, for all the afternoon a cruel high cold wind had been raising dust-clouds around us, and buffeting us till we could hardly get on!

During a great part of the march I trotted by my master's side.

The night turned out bitterly cold, and as we lay on the ground the rain fell in torrents. The thunder roared and lightning flashed, till I thought surely we would be all drowned. As it was we were drenched to the skin.

Firing took place next morning, and I was a bit frightened; but Jock told me the men were only firing off their pieces to make sure they were all right, after the heavy night of drenching rain.

The fight was to begin to-day, this very forenoon, for the enemy with all his guns was but five miles away, in his fortified camp at Brásjòon.

" The fur would soon fly," said Cracker, beginning to get much interested.

"Ah! but, Cracker, the fur didn't fly, for the enemy did."

" They weren't real terriers," Cracker said, "you bet."

No, and so they ran, and we took their camp, and their guns, and a lot of other things, and settled down for a bit, after destroying all the stores we didn't want.

It was a cold, clear night, with the moon shining very brightly on the plain and camp, and on the great mountains rising in rocky terraces high into the starry sky, and not very far from us. We expected the great battle would be fought next day, at least the men said so, and I listened eagerly to all their conversation.

But the fur didn't fly next day after all, and now we set out to walk back to Bushire, after doing the enemy's camp all the damage we could. We started on the march towards the shore at eight o'clock, and marched on and on, singing and talking till midnight came.

Then, Cracker, the fun commenced, and the fur did begin to fly at last.

" Tell us! Tell us!" cried Cracker.

Oh, it is evident, Cracker, you are not a soldier's dog, else you would know that no single person can see more than a very little bit of a battle, although he may be right in the midst of it. But if I didn't see much I heard plenty.

It was sometime past midnight, and the moon was shining, though sand was blowing and getting into our eyes, when shouting and yelling, and awful firing was heard in

the rear of our army.   In less than half-an-hour the moonlight battle was raging its very fiercest.   Horsemen were
galloping here and there, yelling forth words of command,
big guns roared out on the night air, bugles rang, and
musketry roared, and fire flashed in every direction.

Of course, Cracker, being only a cat, I was terribly afraid,
and sometimes I could not see my dear master at all for
the smoke, only his flashing sword ; but I often heard his
brave voice high above the din of the battle, and this gave
me courage and hope.

But my greatest trial came when the wild horsemen of
the enemy came dashing on towards the Highlanders, and
attempted to break their ranks.

Even at this terrible moment poor Jock McNab put up
his hand and smoothed me.

"Hold on, pussy," he said.   "Dinna be feared.   The
tulzie will soon be ower when the grim-faced foreigners
get a taste o' Highland steel."

And a terrible tulzie that was, Cracker, and I saw much
blood, and flashing of fire and steel, and cries and groans
and shrieks.   Oh, it was awful !

Then the heat of the fight seemed to surge away
from us, and Jock found time to put up his hand once
more and say,

"Are ye still there, Shireen ?   Bravo ! pussy."

The firing of the foe was much farther away now, and
kept on thus all night long, till day at length broke pink
and blue over the lovely snow-clad mountains.

Since the fierce raging of the battle, all throughout the
cold hours of night, we had lain where we had stood, without fire or without covering, and showing never a light.
But away in the West the pale moon began to sink at last

in a cloudy haze, and at daylight nothing could be seen
for the grey mists that covered hills and plain.

Master came round and I rose to meet him. He asked
Jock McNab as he smoked and patted my head, whether I
had shown any fear during the fight.

"Never a morsel, sir," said Jock ; "any more than yourself, sir."

Master went back to his place smiling at Jock's way
of paying a compliment.

The firing of the enemy had by this time slackened,
and it was greatly feared by our fine soldier lads that they
had drawn off, and not waited "to get their licks," as
Jock phrased it.

Breakfast was now hastily served out, I sharing with
master, who had come round and sat down beside Jock
and me.

Then by degrees the morning mists gathered up and
up, till they lay only like a grey cloud on the snow-clad
mountain peaks, and we beheld the Persian army drawn
up in battle array ready and waiting for us.

It was a grand sight, Cracker, for the sun now shone
gaily down on their soldiers, in serried ranks of horse
and foot.

They had not long to wait for us, children. But there
was a lot of marching and counter-marching of regiments
and brigades, that I could not understand, unless it was
that our fellows were just showing off their fine clothes.

But the tulzie soon commenced, and as I stuck to my
seat on brave Jock's back, my ears were deafened with
the yelling and shouting and rattling of musketry, and
with the awful roar of the enemy's dread artillery.

On we marched, or rushed, and soon the fight was
almost hand to hand, and so horrible !

But the enemy could not stand the onslaught of our forces. They began to give way and retire, and soon the battle became a rout. The Persians left nearly a thousand dead on the field, and many more bodies lay in every conceivable position along the route they had taken towards the hills.

After our cavalry had chased them afar they returned, and the march was commenced back towards Bushire.

It was a long, cold, wet, and weary one, but we saw the sea at last, and never did soldiers stretch their tired limbs in camp, or make their tea with greater pleasure, than did our poor fellows when they found themselves once more in their entrenched position.

Some of our officers were buried next day, but I was so glad to think that neither my dear master, nor Jock, nor I, were among the wounded.

Jock McNab was loud in his praises of what he was kind enough to call my pluck and coolness in the presence of the foe.

"I wadna gie pussy for onything," he said, "and I'm sure enough she brought us luck, for never a man fell near me, either dead or wounded."

This was my first battle then, Cracker, but it wasn't my last by any means.

As master said, the enemy was beaten, but being beaten doesn't by any means signify that they were conquered.

We remained quiet enough in camp now for many long monotonous days, during which the enemy did not think of disturbing us.

More troops began to arrive from India. The ships lay out yonder at anchor, but a high tumbling sea rolled

in upon the beach, and it was difficult indeed to com-
municate with the vessels, so that the poor horses in
camp began to suffer from hunger, and our own rations
were sometimes scant enough.

The north-west wind too, blew loud and fierce, and
brought with it clouds of dust, and a fine sort of sand that
nothing on earth could keep out of camp. The cold at
night was still bitter, but we had tents now, and I was cosy
enough in master's arms.

They tell me that British soldiers and sailors are born
grumblers. Well, I suppose there is some truth in this;
but I must say, Cracker, our men never grumbled at the
scantiness of their own rations, though they pitied the
horses; but they did grumble a little because the time was
passing on so monotonously, and there seemed no early
chance of having another fight with the Persian foe.

In fact, Cracker, the foe was getting insolent. By night
we now began to see his fires on the hills around, and,
although he had not the courage to attack us, he fired upon
our outposts.

My master, I knew, was getting impatient as well as his
men.

"I want to get farther on up country, pussy," he whispered to me one evening; "up nearer the bonnie woods and
hills where your heart and mine dwell, Shireen, with your
dear mistress Beebee."

I purred and sang, and that seemed to give him heart.

But soon after this Britain's great hero Havelock arrived,
and we all hoped then for a speedy change, and we weren't
disappointed either, Cracker.

"More fur was going to fly, Shireen?"

Yes, dear Cracker, more fur was going to fly, for in a

week or two we were embarked in a transport, and sailing up the Euphrates river to attack the Shah's great army at Mohammerah.

This stronghold was said to be occupied by the very pink and pith of the Persian forces, in number about fifteen thousand in all.

Among the chief regiments behind the formidable earthworks were seven of the Shah's best and bravest. including his guards, and the very flower of his army. Some of these were commanded by a Prince of the blood royal, and somehow or other my master found out that Beebee's father was there also.

When my dear master told me this his eyes were sparkling with joy.

"It is just possible, Shireen," he said, "that Beebee herself may be there, if so——"

He did not finish the sentence, but I knew what he meant.

And now, said Shireen, here come the children, so my little story must end for a time. But you'll come again, won't you, Cracker?

"Oh, like a shot, Shireen," said Cracker, "you bet."

"Oh!" cried Tom, running up. "Come quick, Lizzie. Here is Cracker, the dog that saved Shireen's life, and gave the butcher's bull-terrier such a shaking. Poor doggie Cracker. Poor dear doggie, you won't bite, will you?"

The towsy tyke looked up into the boy's face and wagged his thick, short, stump of a tail at a terrible rate, and there was so much kindness and affection in those brown eyes of his, that Tom at once bent down and threw his arms about his rough and grizzled neck.

Then Lizzie, who had been to fetch some milk, came and placed it down before Cracker.

Cracker really didn't want it, but he drank it rather than anybody should think him ungrateful.

"Mind," said Tom, "you must come to the Castle to-morrow afternoon. It is Shireen's birthday, and we are going to give a party."

Once more Cracker wagged his tail. then he went trotting away to the gate, gave one kindly look behind, and so disappeared.

CHAPTER XVII.

S the weather grew colder, Chammy hugged the fire more, so to speak, and was less and less inclined to run away.

Perhaps to talk of Chammy's pedal progression as "running" is slightly to exaggerate. But, nevertheless, when Chammy made up his mind to go anywhere, whether it were on an expedition to the top of a curtain, or the extreme point of a poplar-tree, he got there all the same. He would probably take a considerable time to make up his mind about it, however, and he would focus the spot he meant to reach with one eye for an hour or two to begin with. Probably, during this survey, his other eye would be wandering all round the room at Shireen, at Warlock, or at Lizzie and Tom. With one eye he was calculating the height of his ambition, as it were, with the other he was counting the chances there were against his ever reaching it at all. These chances had to be reckoned with, for first and foremost he had to descend from his perch or the branch in the ingle-nook. Having reached the floor, he would have to make for the wall of the room and creep along by the foot of the dado, perhaps changing colour once or twice so as to match the hue of the carpet, and thus do his best to escape observation. : For Tabby might be there, and might sing out to Warlock :

"Oh, Warlock, here is Chammy just racing off as fast as lightning. Let us have some fun with him, and turn him over and over a few times."

And they would do it too. And, although the cat and dog meant no harm, their attentions were somewhat disconcerting, to say the very least of it.

Or Lizzie and Tom might be on the floor and spy him, and Lizzie call to Tom, saying,

"Oh, Tom, here is poor Chammy. I'm sure he is cold. Let us take him and nurse him by the fire a little."

And Lizzie might roll him in a Shetland-wool shawl, and sit down before the blaze to warm him, shawl and all, being very much astonished, perhaps, when she opened the shawl to have a peep, to find no Chammy there at all.

"Oh, Tom! Tom!" she would say, looking half afraid, "I'm sure I had Chammy in my hands, and I'm sure I rolled him up ; and now, why, he is clean gone !"

Or the cockatoo might see him, if Uncle Ben were there, and raise a terrible alarm, shrieking and crying, "Scray! Scray! Scray!" till all the prismatic crystals in the old-fashioned chandelier jingled to the sound.

Or the Colonel himself might find him.

"Oh, you're on the hop, are you?" the Colonel would say. "Now you just come back to your perch by the ingle-nook."

And he would lift him by the crest that was over his head and carry him back to the branch.

Chammy was a good-tempered kind of a chameleon at most times, though he could bite a little, and give a good pinch too if he saw any occasion ; but there was nothing in the world made him more indignant than being lifted up by the crest.

It was a handy way of lifting him certainly, but Chammy used to get pea-green with anger when you did so, and his little nimble eyes would look directly back at you ; or, I should rather say, one of them would, for very seldom indeed did he send them both to duty at the same time.

"Put me down at once, sir," he would say, or seem to say, "this is an indignity I do not feel called upon tamely to submit to. You would not dare to lift a croco-dile of the Nile thus. Yet I, too, belong to the ancient family of the Saurians, and I bid you beware."

I have said that Chammy could bite. This is true ; but if the weather were extra cold, he would stand any amount of teasing rather than be bothered, turning his head or opening his mouth to pinch you. One of Chammy's mottoes was " *Pereverantia vincit* " (Perseverance overcomes), and if his master put him back on his perch a hundred and fifty times after he, Chammy, had made up his mind to reach the top of that curtain, or get out at the window to climb a tree, he would watch his chance, bide his time, and begin all over again.

That is the sort of chameleon Chammy was.

The deliberation manifested in all the droll animal's movements was something to watch and wonder at, and afforded no end of amusement to Lizzie and Tom. He never lifted more than one leg at a time. Not he. Four legs in four seconds. That was the speed of his pedal progression, and you didn't need a stop-watch either to determine it. But he studied periodically on the march. He might be slow, but he was also wondrous sure, and when it came to the turn of say a left hind leg, to move it had to come to time, else Chammy would slightly turn his head and focus one goggle backwards, as much as to say:

" What's the hitch along down there? Why on earth don't you move instead of delaying the procession? "

When Chammy saw a fly that he had taken a fancy to, he would stalk cautiously along towards it, one leg at a time of course, and if the fly was fool enough to wait there long enough, why, it got caught and swallowed, that was all. If it didn't, why Chammy evinced no great degree of disappointment, another fly would be sure to come. Everything comes to the chameleon who waits. So he would wait.

There was a deal to be done, mind you, before a fly could be caught. He must first judge the distance, being well acquainted with the length of his own tongue. Then the jaws began to open, which they did as slowly as the minute hand of a watch. After the jaws were opened and both goggles focussed, the tongue, which looked like a garden snail, went slowly straight out. Pop! Where is the fly? And where is the tongue? Well, the tongue went back like a bit of india-rubber, and evidently the fly was there too, for Chammy immediately began to move his jaws like a cow chewing the cud, only infinitely slower.

When flies were scarce, Lizzie or Tom fed Chammy with mealworms. They would take up one at a time with a pair of forceps and put it on Chammy's plate.

Chammy's plate, by the way, was the lid of a pill-box,

and sometimes he would eat a dozen good big fat meal-worms at one sitting, and perhaps refuse food for ten days or more after it.   If presented with a mealworm when not hungry, Chammy would focus it with one eye for about a dozen seconds, then slowly turn his head away in the drollest manner possible.

" Excuse me," he would seem to say, " but I couldn't touch it.   No good eating if you're not hungry, is there? Take it away.   Take it away."

Chammy's attitudes were droll in the extreme while on his tree-branch.   Sometimes he would be quite perpendicular against a topmost twig, which he held for all the world as an old, old man holds his long staff, his chin resting on his two clasped hands.   When he had warmed both his hands at the fire on a wintry day, he used to slowly turn round his back to the blaze to entice a little heat into his chilly old spine.

But Chammy got many a tumble, and sometimes he would stupidly catch his own tail to prevent himself from falling.   So that if he had lived for hundreds of years, and he certainly gave one that impression, he had not gained a very great amount of wisdom in that time.

But he was wise enough to know that the flies were to be found mostly on the window panes, though for the life of him he never could discover why he couldn't catch one when it was on the other side of the glass.   He would have a shot at such a fly again and again, then turn pea-green with anger and disappointment, and crawl slowly away.

The Colonel was a very humane man, and when the frost became very hard, he placed a small but elegant oil-stove in a corner for the comfort of the chameleon.   It had crimson glass in front, and as this glass got warm, Chammy used to stand up against it, the whole forming a very pretty picture.

Then Lizzie got a box and lined it with red flannel, and Chammy was put to bed in it every night. But the oil-stove had to be lit before he could be prevailed upon to stir of a morning. When Chammy felt certain, from his feelings, that the room was well-aired, then he gathered himself slowly up and took up a position on the edge of the box and in the front of the stove, and there he stood for hours, warming first one hand and then another.

Well, I have been writing about this queer pet all the time as if it had been a male. But the truth is, it turned out to be as Tommie said, a " her chameleon," for lo! and behold it was discovered one morning that Chammy had laid some eggs. She put them all together in a heap in the corner and appeared to be employed all the time lifting and counting them and feeling them over. There were five altogether, about the size and shape of small beans, and pink in colour.

Chammy ate no food after this. She didn't even seem to care to come any more to warm her toes at the stove. And, on going to take off the lid of her box one morning, Lizzie found poor Chammy immovable and colder than ever she had been before.

Then Lizzie sat down on the floor beside the red-lined box and burst into tears.

    *   •   *

They made Chammy a grave near the sweet-scented syringa-tree, and when springtime came, they planted it with forget-me-nots, and Chammy never came again.

CHAPTER XVIII.

HIREEN'S birthday party at the Castle was going to be a very grand affair, so Tommy and Lizzie would have told you, for they had made great preparations for celebrating the event.

Shireen had reached the advanced age of one-and-twenty, and yet there was but little sign that her strength was actually failing her. She did not care to move about quite so much as she had done many years before, and preferred, as we have seen, to take her little rambles about the village, and visit her many friends there.

She preferred, too, the lawn to the forest on a sunny summer's afternoon, or a seat by the low fire among her old friends, when the wintry winds were roaring around the chimneys, and shaking doors and windows.

But to look at Shireen, with her lovely coat, her sweet face, her wee, short ears, and blue eyes, you would not have said she was more than seven.

"I wonder," said Lizzie, on the morning of Shireen's birthday, "if Mrs. Cooper will come, and bring her lovely prize cat Stamboul?"

"Oh, yes, she is sure to come," was the reply. "I've just had a letter."

So away ran Lizzie and Tom to complete the arrangements for the afternoon and evening entertainment, for the great *coup de théâtre* was to consist of lighting up the grounds after dark with coloured lamps, and the flower-beds and borders with fairy lights, and this duty devolved upon Lizzie and her little brother.

How anxiously they scanned the sky as they hung up their lamps and their Chinese lanterns, and how suspiciously they eyed the clouds, I need not tell you. But twenty times, at least, Tom ran to ask his uncle if he was quite sure it wouldn't rain. So at last Uncle Clarkson told him that he was only a soldier, and not supposed to be able to read the signs or the sky, and that if they wanted true information, they must go to old Ben ; they might as well bring him to luncheon. So, as soon as everything had been completed to the entire satisfaction of the children, off they set, and in a little more than an hour's time, they re-appeared again, dragging Uncle Ben by his two hands on to the lawn.

Luncheon was laid in a tent erected specially for the purpose, and some time before they all sat down, a carriage rattled up the avenue, and Mrs. Cooper herself alighted with her maid, who was carrying a mysterious-looking parcel, which was half basket, half bird's cage, and really was the travelling-home of Stamboul, the prize cat.

Everyone waited anxiously to see Stamboul, and when presently he stalked forth, with his lovely red and white coat shining like satin and floating all over him, there was a general hum of admiration.

Stamboul did not take very much notice of anyone. He gave one glance at Shireen, then looked at the dogs. Satisfying himself, apparently, that they were harmless, he next turned his attention to the grass, walking gingerly over it, and shaking a fore-foot at every step, in case it might be damp.

Then he entered the tent and disposed of himself in a straw chair, that had a cushion to it.

Now, although the party congregated together to celebrate Shireen's birthday was everything that could be desired, and though the feast was fit for a queen, and the lawn and grounds after dark looked like a scene from the "Arabian Nights," still it is more with the cats and dogs we have to do than with Lizzie's and Tom's little human friends, or the older human beings who sat in the tent, talking and laughing very pleasantly indeed.

Shireen and her old friends occupied a beautifully lit up summer-house. Even Cracker and the chameleon, who at this time was alive, were here to-night; but Stamboul occupied the place of honour, which was a straw chair, and he accepted the dignity with the easy grace of a prince of the blood royal, and as if he quite merited the honour and dignity.

For some time he sat thoughtfully washing his beautiful face, and all kept silence around him, till he should be pleased to break the silence.

"Yes, Shireen," he said at last, "I have been a prize cat now for many years, and, indeed, I believe I am entitled to dub myself a champion.   Oh, no, Mr. Warlock," he continued, smiling, "I wasn't always a prize cat; nor have I been all my life as beautiful and fully pelaged as I am now; indeed, I was once as plain and humble-looking as your friend Tabby there."

Tabby winced and felt a little hurt. Certainly she did not lay claim to any great degree of beauty; still it seemed hard she should be thus singled out.

Even Chammy turned one eye down at her, and Dick cocked a black bead of an optic towards her. Only Warlock gave her face a kind of consolatory lick, as much as to say,

"If you ain't very pretty, Tabby, you are very good, and virtue is better, any day, than beauty."

"Well, my friends," continued Stamboul, "you may think it is very nice to be a first-prize cat, and to be made a great fuss with, and a great show of at exhibitions, and to be boasted about by your mistress, and crowed over by her friends; but I can tell you a show cat's life has its dark side as well as its light, and this, I think, you will be ready enough to admit, when you have heard some of my adventures and experiences."

STAMBOUL'S LIFE AND CAREER.

"Ever see a cattery, Shireen? No, I dare say you never did; and of course, Tabby, you never did? Well, I will tell you of the cattery in which I was born, and there are many far less pleasant than that, I can assure you.

"I remember it well, though it is many years ago. I don't say that I can actually recollect the day of my birth, but I mind the days of my kittenhood right well. And I can remember as if it were but yesterday, the morning I and my brothers and sisters were all bundled off to a show."

"To be sold, I suppose?" said Shireen.

"Yes, my dear," said Stamboul, "to be sold. But mind

you, I don't blame my old mistress in the least for this. She was at heart a lover of animals ; and if she kept us in a cattery, and restricted us of our liberty to some extent, it was not altogether her fault.

"Mrs. Rayne was a widow lady, and lived almost by herself in a pretty house in the country. She had neither kith nor kin belonging to her, as far as ever I could see. She had one faithful old man-servant and his wife, who lived in the house and attended on her in every way. But Mrs. Rayne looked after the cattery herself. She fed us, and she gave us milk and water."

" Thought cats never drank water ? " said Cracker.

" A very great mistake, I assure you, sir," said Stamboul. " A cat won't thrive unless she has water, and that water must be soft, and clean, and sweet."

" Well, Stamboul,' Cracker said, " a dog is never too old to learn."

" But," continued Stamboul, " I must tell you about the cattery. You see, there was a little cottage down in the grounds, nicely shaded with trees and all that, and with oceans of honeysuckle swelling all over the porch, and clustering round the windows. It was only a two-roomed cottage ; but, nevertheless, Mrs. Rayne conceived the notion of turning it into a cattery, for this amiable lady had an idea that if she did her best to improve the breed of cats in this country, she would be able to get for them a somewhat higher place or standing as members of society.

" She had commenced by keeping a few—three I think — for her own pleasure ; but one by one they disappeared. They had been trapped, poisoned, or shot by the keepers, so she saw that if she were to do any good at all, she must protect her valuable cats, and at the same time keep their

breed and species select and pure. So she had a look
round the cottage one day, and was glad to find, to
commence with, that it was not damp. Dampness in a
cattery is likely to give rise, directly or indirectly, to many
ailments incidental to cat-life.

" Then Mrs. Rayne proceeded to furnish the cottage, after
a fashion, plainly and well. This, I may tell you, Mr.
Cracker, was quite as much for her own sake as for the
sake of the pussies. You see, she reasoned thus, and very
rightly too, cats have become like dogs, domesticated, they
have for countless ages given up their own wild life in the
woods, and hills, and cairns, and elected to live with
mankind, and share his joys and sorrows. In doing so,
they give up, in a great measure, their freedom ; they
become the willing slaves of man, the playmates of his
children, the gentle, soothing comforters to many a lonely
human being, who has nothing before him in this world
except the grave. Well, then, if pussy has done and does
do all this, is it fair to keep her all her little life like a
wild beast, shut up in a cage, or banished to barn or
outhouse ?

" No, and Mrs. Rayne—although the cottage would
be the home of the cats *par excellence*—would often visit it
and spend many an hour therein, with her books or her
knitting. She would even take her food there sometimes,
for a cat never looks upon any place as an ideal home if a
kettle never sings upon a hob by the fire, or a table is
never spread for breakfast, or for tea.

" So, when completed, the cottage not only had a nice
low fire, protected by a strong guard, to be put on when
the fire was lit and no one in the room, but there were in
it a table and stools, a couch, and a nice wicker easy-chair
and footstool.

"There was a cupboard or two also, and there were brackets and flower-stands, and a mirror or two, and nick-nacks on the mantelpiece as well.

"In fact, this room—which was the winter end of the cottage—was so comfortable, that no one could have told it was a cattery. The other room was furnished as a summer-room, and needed no fireplace.

"There was in each a sanitary box of earth; but as the cats had at all times free access to the garden by means of a little swinging door at the bottom of the main door, this box was never used except for the convenience of young kittens.

"You will now observe, Tabby, that Mrs. Rayne, in a manner, lived among her cats, so that she had their companionship and they had hers. Moreover, as a special treat, she used to take one of them into the house, frequently of a night, and whenever any cat was ailing she treated it as kindly and considerately as if it had been a baby.

"The cat's garden itself deserves a word or two.

"You see, galvanized wire fencing is very cheap, as I dare say you, Cracker, being a farmer's dog, know. Well, Mrs. Rayne, first and foremost, laid out the pussies' garden in front of and partly round the cottage. She laid down a bit of a lawn; she planned walks, and planted shrubs and flowers, for I can assure you, Cracker, we cats have an eye for colour and effect as well. Then she surrounded the whole with a high wire fence, covering in the top as well, so that birds might not come in to eat pussies' food, and be eaten by the pussies in turn.

"The place was sheltered from the east and north by a wooden fence, so on the whole, either in winter or in summer, a more comfortable cattery never existed to my knowledge, and I have seen a few.

"The garden was laid out then partly for effect, but partly, also, for utility and luxury. The lawn was a delightful place for the young cats to tumble and jump upon, when the spring and summer were in their prime, and the grass and weed-tops, that grew on this wildery of a lawn, helped to keep the cats in health.

"Then here and there, at different heights all round the wooden fence, and the wire fence also, were placed shelf-seats, about eighteen inches long, by one foot broad. On these the cats would lie and sun themselves, or they could take exercise all round, by leaping from one to the other.

"Among the flowers that grew around was Valerian, of which the cat is fond, and several other pretty flowers, that appealed to pussy's sense of smell, and gratified her eye.

"There was a filter indoors, and large, clean dishes were placed on the floor for the drinking water, so that the furry inmates could help themselves whenever they pleased."

"And a bit of brimstone in each dish, I suppose?" said Cracker. "A fine thing brimstone, you bet."

"Fiddlesticks!" said Stamboul disdainfully. "Mr. Cracker, I am afraid your notions are somewhat antiquated."

"I don't know what that be," retorted Cracker. "I just speak as I've been taught."

"True, true, my good fellow, and doubtless with the best intentions; but then, living in the country as you do, one is bound to believe a great many popular and foolish fallacies."

"I own to it, I own to it, Stamboul," said Cracker.

"Now up north, where I comes from, a cat ain't looked upon as much of a stunner I 'ssure you, Stamboul. They are just kept as a kind o' live mousetraps."

"Yes, I know," said Stamboul; "and they are starved under the mistaken notion that this makes them catch mice."

"So they be. And doesn't it? I know if I were main hungry, and spotted a fine fat rabbit dashing past, I'd soon have he, you bet, and my dinner next, afore he were cold."

"True, Cracker, but it is also a fact that the better a cat is fed, so long as he is not foolishly pampered and spoiled, the better a hunter he will make. You see, Cracker, to catch mice and rats, a cat has to have a deal of patience, and a world of cunning, and spend long nights of determined watching. To do this he must be in form. If he is half-starved, he is nervous, and tired, and weary; if he be hungry, then instead of watching by the cat's run, he'll be thinking more of the cupboard and the last square meal he had, and wondering when he will have another. Or, it is possible enough, instead of watching at all for master rat—and a well-bred cat won't eat a rat after all—he will prefer to do his hunting in the nearest pigeon-loft or hen-house."

"There is a deal in what you say," said Shireen.

"Yes, I can see that," Warlock put in.

"Well,' said Cracker, "I gives in to superior judgment."

"And now," continued Cracker, "is it true, Stamboul, that cats will suck a child's breath? Mind, I'm not so far left to myself as to believe this, although there, maybe is, some hayseed in my hair."

"A sillier notion," said Stamboul, "was never heard,

and this fallacy dates back to the days of witchcraft. Pah! out on such a ridiculous notion, it is really too absurd to argue about."

"Well, Lady Shireen there, while telling her story, has proved in her own experience that it isn't places so much that cats love as persons," said Tabby.

"That is true, Tabby, if the persons are good to them; and I really think that people are beginning to think now, that cats are reasoning, thinking beings, with minds differing from their own only in degree."

"If not interrupting you too much, Stamboul," said Warlock, "I have just one word to say, having been a student of cat-life, especially of Mother Shireen there, and my own companion and field-ranger, honest Tabby here. Well, there is a saying, which is all too common among human beings I think, and that is the expression, 'As cross as a cat.' I've seen a cat cross, and I've felt her claws, too, but that was when she was either done out of her rights and starved, or put upon in some way or another."

"Glad to hear you stick up for cats, Warlock," said Stamboul.

"Oh, I just speak of cats as I find them. Now, for instance, who is it among human beings I wonder, that hasn't noticed how fond a well-trained, well-kept cat is of children?

"Here is a bit master read in a book the other day, and he told me that the writer had studied cats ever since he was the height of the parlour tongs.*

"'But,' says the author, 'the domestic cat is *par*

---

* 'The Domestic Cat," by same author.

N

excellence the playmate and friend of childhood. What is
it, indeed, that pussy will not bear from the hands of its
child-mistress? She may pull and lug pussy about any
way she pleases, or walk up and down the garden-walk
with it slung over her shoulder by the tail. If such treatment does hurt the poor cat, she takes good care not to
show it. It is amusing enough sometimes to watch a little
girl making a baby of her favourite pussy. They are
wearied with gambolling together on the flowery lawn, and
playing at hide-and-seek among the shrubbery, and pussy
"*must* be tired," says little Alice. Pussy enters into the
joke at once, and seems positively dead beat; so the
basket is brought, the little nightcap is put on, the shawl
is carefully pinned around its shoulders, and this embryo
mamma puts her feline baby to bed and bids it sleep.
There are always two words, however, with pussy as regards
the sleeping part of the contract, for little Alice never can
get her baby to close more than one eye at a time. Pussy
must see what is going on. Anon the baby "must be
sick," and pussy forthwith appears as if she couldn't
possibly survive another hour. Bread pills are manufac-
tured, and forced down the poor cat's throat, she barely
resisting. Then lullabies, low and sweet, are sung to her,
which pussy enjoys immensely, and presently, joining in
the song herself, goes off to sleep in earnest.

"'And Alice, pussy's friend, although at times she may
use the furry favourite rather roughly, is kind to her in the
main. Doesn't pussy get a share of Alice's porridge every
morning? Doesn't she sup with Alice every night? And
do you think for one moment that Alice would go to bed
without her of a night? Not she! And still this cat
may be as savage as a tiger to strangers, and even to

those in the house who do not treat her well. And let anyone else, except a child, attempt to lift this pussy by the tail, and see what he will see.'"

"And feel what he'll feel," said Cracker; "and serve him right, says I."

"But I fear," said Shireen, "this is somewhat of a digression. You were talking, Stamboul, of your pleasant and delightful cattery, the home of your kittenhood."

"Yes. Well, I shall go on with my story."

CHAPTER XIX.

 " HE cattery then," continued Stamboul, "in which I was born, was really a very pleasant home, chiefly I think from the fact that dear old Mrs. Rayne studied our ways and habits. She didn't stint us in food either."

"Gave you plenty of fish, I suppose?" said Cracker.

"Well," said Stamboul, smiling, "I do not deny that cats do like a bit of fish; but, bless you, my dear Cracker, it is a mistake to think they don't like flesh far better."

"Mrs. Rayne had no less than seven female or queen cats, and two beautiful Toms. One of these lived in the house constantly and was Mrs. Rayne's especial favourite. He was my dear father, but, alas! like many a beautiful cat, he got caught in a trap one day, and came home with a terribly lacerated leg. It got better for a time, but in his struggle no doubt, my father had hurt himself internally, for he became sickly after this, grew thin, and lost all appetite. Then his coat fell off in patches, and one day he was missing.

"Yes, he was· found again, but dead. He had only

gone down the garden, feeling, I suppose, that his end was near, and crept in under the dark shade of a bush to die.

" But the secret of Mrs. Rayne's success in rearing nice cats with wondrous coats, just like mine and yours, Shireen, was this—she fed her pussies with regularity and gave them plenty of variety of course. A little porridge and milk was our regular breakfast, but there was some variety as regards the dinner every day. Nor did she forget that cats like a little nicely-mashed greens now and then, and even a bit of tomato and any other raw fruit and vegetable, if it be but a potato paring."

" Many cats many tastes, I suppose," said Warlock.

" That's it, Warlock, you speak like a book ; but then you have enjoyed the not slight privilege of having had a cat as a companion, the cat being the superior animal."

Cracker looked at Warlock and Warlock looked at Cracker, and I rather think their thoughts were very similar, only they said nothing. It wouldn't have been polite.

" Well, my friends," said Stamboul, "such was the home in which I was born and reared up to the age of two months. Then the show came round.

" Mrs. Rayne said that we—the four kittens—were all very, very beautiful and fascinating, and that if her purse were only half as big as her heart she would not part with one of us. ' However,' she added, ' those who buy you must pay your price, and having done so, they will value you all the more.'

" So mother and I were placed in a nice roomy box, not a wretched little reticule of a thing such as I have more than once travelled in to cat shows. The guard was warned to take precious care of us, and so he did.

"Mrs. Rayne was at the station to meet us herself, and conveyed us in a cab all the way to the show.

"We were in good time, so that our dear mistress had an opportunity of arranging our pen for us before putting us in, and also to speak a bit of her mind to the manager and promoter.

"'The pens are too small, Mr. Silk,' she said.

"'Very sorry indeed, madam,' said Mr. Silk.

"'Yes, but sorrow will hardly give the poor pussies any more room.'

"'Then there is no sanitary box of earth placed behind each pen, and you, Mr. Silk, ought to know that a well-trained cat is the most cleanly animal on earth. Why don't you take a lesson from Mr. Cruft?'

"'I'll have that seen to another year.'

"'Thank you, Mr. Silk, and now will you have the goodness to send me a man to sweep out that abominable sawdust from my cat's pen?'

"'The sawdust, madam! Why surely——'

"'I said the sawdust. Nothing worse could be imagined. It gets in the cat's fur. It gets in their milk, and if they have a morsel of meat, that also is rolled in it, and they are probably half poisoned.'*

"Having had the sawdust removed, Mrs. Rayne put down our pretty cushions, gave us a little warm milk sweetened with sugar, patted our mother, and left.

"The judging was over by the time she returned, and she was very pleased to note, that she had won first prize for the cat and first for the kittens.

"Mother was half asleep, but we—the kittens—were

* This, however, was properly arranged at Mr. Cruft's great Aquarium Cat Show of 1894.

lively enough and full of tricks and fun. There was quite a crowd of well-dressed people around our pen watching our gambols, and so Mrs. Rayne was not surprised to be told soon afterwards by the secretary, that two of her kittens were claimed at catalogue prices.

"Mrs. Rayne sighed. She would just as soon have taken us all home again, she said.

"Well, my friends, I sigh when I think of my pleasant home with Mrs. Rayne, and I think I see the dear old lady now, with her snow-white hair and sunny smile. I never saw my country home again, and I never saw my mistress more. But a cat that I met at a show the other day, and got conversing with in the evening when all the people had gone, told me that she had come from Mrs. Rayne's cattery, which was now no more, they having carried the old lady to her grave a year ago. Heigho! there is a deal of sorrow in this world to cats as well as men.

"Well, at the first show we were all sold to different owners. I never knew where my brothers and sisters went, but I live in hopes of some day meeting them at a show.

"That first show was not a well-conducted one, and though it was held at the Crystal Palace, the cages were placed in a draughty place, and the pens they told me at another show, to which I was sent afterwards, had been used for other animals. I don't know how this may be; but I do know that something was wrong, for nearly a score of cats at that show caught infectious ailments, which speedily carried them off after they got home.

"Alas! my friends, I was now to have a new experience, and one of a very painful nature. I had been bought, not

by anyone to keep as a pet, but by a woman—I cannot say
lady—who kept cats for profit and profit alone. She
had no love for them, all she expected was to pocket gain
by them.

"My heart sunk when I was taken into this filthy
den, for it was nothing else. It was a room in a small
suburban cottage, and contained no less than twenty cats
and kittens of all breeds and ages. Many of these were
confined in cages of the most crampy and filthy kind.

"The poor inmates indeed seemed in a woeful plight.

"I got talking to one of them in an adjoining berth
to my own after it was dark.

"'I suppose,' I said innocently, 'I shall soon be taken to
a real home?'

"'A real home!' said the silver tabby I had addressed.
'Well, you may, but I very much doubt it. Why, some of
us have been in this dismal prison for three long years,
and may be for years and years again, unless we have the
luck to die or to get sold, for escape seems impossible.
We are kept for breeding.

"'You are well fed, I suppose?'

"'Well fed? Ah! you'll soon know how we are fed.
Why, we never get a change of any kind; it is milk and
bread, milk and bread and half putrid lumps of horse-
flesh from one month's end to another, and never a blade
of grass to cool our blood and to refresh us. And we only
have one little run in the backyard yonder once a day,
when mistress happens not to be busy elsewhere.'

"'Yet, nevertheless,' continued my informant, 'mistress is
supposed to be a celebrated breeder, and sometimes a lady
arrives at the door of her cottage and is shown into a
nicely-furnished room. She has come most likely to buy

a cat or kitten. We are all kept groomed and ready
always, and not having any exercise, we are moderately
plump and fat. Well, soon after the carriage stops, mistress herself, better dressed than usual, hurries in and
picks up one of us, and takes a brush and comb and goes
rapidly over the coat. Then she enters the best room,
petting and hugging the poor pussy. Ah! well does
the cat know that it is all false affection; but she sings
and looks pleasant, the prospect of leaving this vile den
making her happy and hopeful for a time.'

"'And then,' I said, 'when a pussy is sold she is taken
away in the carriage to some pretty and refined home,
where she will be well cared for, and have good food
and toys, and maybe beautiful children to play with, and

"'Like a dream her life will pass away!'"

"'Ah!' sighed the silver tabby, 'would it were so. But
it is far often the reverse.'

"'Indeed!'

"'Yes, and I am going to tell you why. *You see cats
like us, that have been dragged up in a den like this, and
without human companionship, never learn manners. They
are never cleanly in their habits, and just as often thieves as
not. So the new purchaser soon finds out her mistake,
and pussy, instead of becoming a parlour pet, is thrust out of
doors, illused by the servants, and in time becomes a nomad
and helps to swell the great army of vagrant cats, that
commit depredations of every conceivable sort and render
night hideous by their howlings.'

---

* The sentences I place in italics should be remembered by all who think of
buying a beautiful cat for a companion.

"My young heart sunk when I heard this intelligence, and, alas! I soon found it was all too true. Yes, my dear Shireen, and more than true, for not only were all the cats in this great prison-house treated as if they had been wild beasts, but sometimes even with systematic cruelty I myself was soon the subject of this. You see, that having been used to good food in variety, with plenty of fresh air and exercise, I fell ill. I could not drink the thin skimmed-milk, and I loathed the high half-putrid horse-flesh. Then my skin became irritable. So one day my mistress hauled me out of my cage and slapped me across the head till my eyes grew almost blind, and I was dizzy.

"'I shall lose by you, confound you,' she cried.

"Then I was taken to a dirty back kitchen and scrubbed, yes, literally scrubbed with hot water and soap, then roughly dried and put in a cage near the fire. When half dry I was smeared all over with some vilely-smelling ointment till I loathed the very smell of myself. After this I was put in the hospital cage in another room. Here there was a cat in a worse plight than myself by far.

"She didn't care to talk at all.

"'I'm too sick and ill to speak,' she said. 'Besides, I'm going to be drowned to-night. I do so wish the night was come.'

"I shuddered with horror and fear.

"The night did come, and with it the executioner. He seized my poor companion and thrust her roughly into a sack, in which I could see there were some old bricks. Then he tied her up and left the room.

"I got worse instead of better, and there came a day

when, from something in my mistress's eye, I knew that I too was doomed.

"I received no food or drink of any kind that day ; my inhuman mistress no doubt considering it would be mere waste to give meat to a cat she was going to drown.

"I determined, however, that I would make a struggle for life.

"The day passed wearily by, and how very, very long it did seem to be sure.

"At last—ah ! how my heart did beat—the door of the room opened and the same horrid ragged man came in. He carried a lantern and a sack with bricks, just as before.

"I pretended to be asleep.

"He cautiously opened the door.

"In a moment I sprang up, and he speedily withdrew a badly-bitten hand. Before he could shut me up again I had dashed out and darted from the room.

"I knew not where to run ; but here was a window. I was a powerful kitten for my age.

"So the window flew into flinders and I was free.

"Yes, I was free. A homeless, wretched nomad. Now some cats are possessed of the homing instinct, as it is called, in great perfection. But, alas ! I felt none of it, else you may be sure, my friends, I should have found my way back again speedily enough to Mrs. Rayne's.

"But I was free. Oh, how glad even that thought made me.

"The fresh air blew in my face, and I felt better and stronger already. I glanced up and down the street. Far up one end of it were many lights, the other was all dark and so I chose that.

"I ran on and on and on, and soon found myself in the

country, and tired at last, I crept into a shed and went to sleep among some clean hay, the fragrant smell of which seemed to curl round my heart and revive me.

"I was hungry when daylight came, and was lucky enough to find a mouse, on which I breakfasted, and then went to sleep again.

"It was dark when I awoke, and so I resumed my journey, still going in the same direction, guided by some instinct to place as great a distance as possible 'twixt myself and the cat-dealer's den I had escaped from.

"Before daylight I came to a great forest, and being tired, I crept in under a bush of furze, and, on a warm dry bed, slept long and sweetly.

"I idled about the forest all night—and a lovely moonlit night it was—finding plenty of food, but seeing no men and no dogs.

"I determined, therefore, to make this forest my home for a time, at all events; but I must not sleep on the ground, for dogs would be sure to find me out and worry me. Luckily I found a comfortable shelter half way up the trunk of a grand old oak, and so I concluded to live here. And a most perfect shelter I found it to be.

"For many, many months, I could not tell you, my friends, how many, I lived in this tree, becoming entirely nocturnal in my habits, for when I ventured out during the day I sometimes saw rough-looking men with dogs, and was glad to escape into the branches of some oak or beech, where I sat trembling with fear until they had gone.

"I found plenty of food in the forest, and my drink was the pure soft water from the purling brooklets. The only thing I ever did long for was a drop of milk.

"The summer and autumn passed away, and winter came wild and dreary. The birds no longer sang in the forests, and many had flown south and away to summer lands beyond the seas. I missed many of my forest friends too ; they had gone away, or had hidden them-selves in cosy corners and gone to sleep for the winter. This kind of long sleep was denied to me however, and now I often felt cold and wretched, and would wander for hours through the snow and under the stars or moon, that used to glimmer down through the leafless branches, and fall in patches of light on the ground beneath.

"One evening, while wandering thus, I came upon a little country cottage, and, listening near to the stackyard, I heard the voice of a young girl raised in song coming from one of the outhouses.

"I crept nearer and nearer, and presently came to the door of the byre, where the cows were. The girl's song was a very simple and a very sweet one ; but far more sweet to me was the sound of the purling milk as it fell in rich streams into the pail.

"The temptation to enter was irresistible. But I did not venture too far in.

"'Oh, what a pretty pussy!' said the girl.

"Her voice re-assured me, and I began to sing. She tried to get me to come indoors with her, but I was too wild and suspicious for that. Yet I accompanied her as far as the cottage door, and I even peeped in.

"A cheerful fire of wood was burning on the hearth. How pleasant it looked! And near it sat an old man smoking, and two pretty children—a girl and a boy— were playing by the fireside.

"They brought me bread and milk, and I ate it coyly

and hungrily. But when they would have taken me up
I ran out again, and once more made for the forest,
and for my cold bed in the tree.

" Next night, however, I returned to the cottage, and
was treated with equal kindness; and so for night after
night, till the children used to quite expect me. I allowed
them to smooth and pat me now, and sometimes I went
indoors and sat a little by the fire.

" But one dark and stormy evening some dogs and
men discovered my tree. They had traced me by my
footprints through the snow.

" It was, however, too late for them to do anything
to me that night, but I knew they would come and rout
me out when morning broke, so I made up my mind now
that the forest was no longer safe for me in winter. That
night I left the tree, and wandering away to the cottage,
I took shelter in the outhouse above the room where
the cows dwelt.

" Next morning I astonished and delighted the children
by appearing among them to breakfast. I had captured a
huge rat, and, bringing it in with me, I laid it on the
hearth to show my prowess. By so doing I quite ingra-
tiated myself with the old man.

" And so it ended by my taking up my abode with
these good people.

" When summer came again I used to go roving in
the forest, for a very delightful life I found it. Nevertheless, I invariably came home in the evening, and did
my best to keep the outhouse clear of rats and the rooms
indoors free from the plague of mice.

" I was a great favourite with this humble family,
and many people came from afar to see the wonderful

wild cat as they called me, who had been tamed by the power of kindness.

" I loved the old man, and used to sit on his knee of an evening, as he sat and smoked his short clay pipe by the fire ; and I loved the children too, especially little Alfred, the boy who would never go to bed at night until I was ready to go with him.

" Poor wee fellow, he fell ill at last, and this was the beginning of the end of life in the grand old forest.

" Alfred died, and they took him away to his long home, and I never saw him more. But I used often and often in the bright summer days to go and sit on his little grave and think of him. People said I expected he would one day come again. Nothing of the sort. Cats know what death is, and I felt sure that Alfred would never, never come again.

" I knew these people were very, very poor, because one day, when a lady came to see the wonderful wild cat and took quite a fancy to me and offered my master a a long price, he reluctantly agreed to part with me.

" He sat silent for a long time.

" But I could see the tears silently coursing down his cheeks.

" Then he turned to the lady.

" 'Take Tim, then,' he said, 'take him and be good to him. He were my wee lad's cat like that be dead and gone, but a ten-poun' note's an' awfu' temptation to poor folks like we, and will get the children many a little comfort for the comin' winter. Pay the lassie,' he added, 'I'll no touch it.'

" He gave one glance at the fireside, and then went out and stayed away for hours.

" He could not bear to see me leave."

CHAPTER XX.

HAND MET HAND IN A HEARTY SHAKE.

 DO not think that Shireen would have been quite happy, had she not been able to go now and then and see her village friends, especially perhaps Emily and the blacksmith.

A rough-looking and a rough-voiced sort of a man was Mr. Burn-the-wind, as the villagers called him ; but it will be readily enough admitted, I think, that there is always some good in people whom cats, and dogs, and children, are fond of. You see, it is like this : we grown-up people are very apt to judge others by their speech, and by what people say about them ; while the children, and the creatures we are so fond of calling the lower animals, read one's character often at a glance, or if not, by one's actions at all events. Well, Mr. Burn-the-wind was actually beloved by dogs and cats, and seldom during the day could you have come into his shop without finding a crowd of merry children there, with whom the good fellow laughed and romped, or chased round and round the anvil.

Lizzie and Tom looked in pretty often to see the blacksmith, although they were what the people called gentlefolks' children, and although Burn-the-wind did not take the liberty of romping with them, he told them many a droll story, and sometimes sang them a song.

Then Shireen used to be found there, and if Tom and Lizzie came in and wa'ted awhile, she went trotting home with them, and sometimes they met Cracker, and so they all came back together.

Tom admired Burn-the-wind very much, and sometimes insisted upon being taken up on his sturdy shoulders, that he might catch hold of the bellows handle and blow the fire And how he used to laugh, to be sure, when the coals got red and hot sparks flew !

" What are you going to be when you grow up ? " said Burn-the-wind one day to Tom.

" I haven't twite (quite) made up my mind yet," replied Tom manfully, ' but I will either be a great general, and cut off lots of heads, or a blacksmith, and soo (shoe) horses."

Tom thought it grand fun to see a horse being shod, and wondered at the animal's patience in holding up foot after foot, while Shireen sat by and sang.

The snow was on the ground one afternoon when Lizzie and Tom, rosy and healthy-looking after a long walk, dropped in on their way home.

Warlock and Tabby were with them, and Vee-Vee also.

" Is Shireen here, Mister Blacksmith ? " said Tom.

" Aye, that she is, my lad. Been singing to me, and I was singing to her. Oh, we're fine friends, I assure you."

So all waited with Burn-the-wind for some time and then all went home together, after bidding the village smith a kindly good-night.

Uncle Ben was just coming out of his gate as they

U

passed, with Cockie on his shoulder, and the bird screamed
with delight when she saw the party.

"Oh, Uncle Ben," cried Lizzie, "you're coming to the
Castle, aren't you ?"

"Yes, my dear, that's where old Ben is bent upon going
for a game of chess and a long clay pipe."

The little party were all assembled to-night around the
low fire, which was burning and spluttering away most
cheerfully. Even Chammy was squatting on a branch of
his tree by the ingle-nook, holding up first one hand and
then another to the welcome blaze.

"Shall I begin just where I left off, Cracker?" said
Shireen.

"Oh, do!" cried Cracker. "I want to hear about more
fur flying, you bet."

Well, then, said Shireen, we left a sufficiently large
army to guard the entrenched camp at Bushire, and went
on with quite a small, and very daring fleet, to attack
the large army of the Shah, in the town of Mohammerah.

I felt somewhat sad after we had reached the fortified town we were going to attack, to find that I was
not to be taken on shore, and so you see, Cracker, I
can give no personal narrative of the battle, because I
was not in the thick of it, and didn't actually see the
fur flying.

But all I saw on the morning of the twentieth of
March impressed me very much. Where do you think
I went for safety, Warlock ?

"Into your master's bed, perhaps."

No, Warlock, but right up into the main-top crosstrees,
where I could be as far as possible away from our own
ship's guns. I had no fear of the enemy's guns.

I had gone up there very early and at daybreak heard much heavy firing, for a raft had been placed quite close to the walls of a fort, with mortars on it. Then soon after all our ships began to batter the walls of the fortified town, and they got as near as possible in order to do this. But mind you, Cracker, the Persians weren't slow at returning the fire, and some of their round shot crashed into our ship, and made her tremble from stem to stern.

"That means from head to tail, doesn't it, Shireen?"

Yes, Cracker. One great shot came tearing quite close past me, but I took no heed. Indeed, despite the roar of battle that was going on on all sides of me, I couldn't help thinking about my mistress. Everything beautiful always made me think of Beebee. And it was a lovely sight I saw.

"The battle?" said Cracker.

Well no, not so much that perhaps, but the morning was bright and clear, every puff of white smoke, with its tongue of fire, made me jump a little, but the smoke itself was borne quickly to leeward on the wings of a cool breeze. Then on shore were the low wicked-looking forts, and the greenery of trees, and the Persian horsemen in splendid uniform dashing hither and thither, and the ships themselves, with the loosely hanging canvas and their flags, on the river, glittering in the rays of the spring sunshine. All was beautiful.

Then further on in the day began the disembarkation, and I saw my dear master among his hilted warriors going on shore, and my heart sank with fear, as I thought he might be shot.

I even began to descend the rigging to go with him,

but then I thought I could be of no use, and so remained.

All the while the troops were leaving, the battle
of great guns raged on between ships and shore, and I
was dreadfully alarmed once at a fearful explosion that
took place on shore, for the enemy's magazine blew up,
and masses of masonry and timber, and mangled human
beings were thrown straight into the air amidst sheets
of flame and rolling clouds of smoke.

Well, Cracker, I did not see my dear master again for
three or four days, and very anxious I was ; but I had
heard that the British arms had been everywhere successful, and that the town and all the forts were in our possession.
The army of the Shah had fled far away.

When my master came back at last, and honest Jock
McNab with him, how loudly I sang as I ran to meet
them ! It was one of the happiest days in my life.

But a strange adventure now gave hope and happiness
to my dear master once more.

One beautiful afternoon there he was, walking on the
ramparts of one of the half-ruined ports of Mohammerah,
in company with Jock McNab, his faithful Scottish servant.
To-day, all being safe, I myself was permitted to come on
shore with them, and I was seated on Jock's shoulder.
After gazing for a short time down into the silver, silent
river—his thoughts, I felt, were very far away—the surgeon
of the ship came round.

"Ah ! Edgar," he said, "have you seen the ruins of the
exploded magazine yet ?"

"No, my friend. Is it worth beholding ?"

"Well, yes, if you are not too nervous. But a sight so
ghastly and awful I have never yet clapped eyes upon."

"I'll go," said master. "Mac, just wait here for me a few minutes."

Jock saluted, and seating himself on a block of masonry, took me off my perch and began to play with me.

While so engaged, a footstep fell upon our ears, and we both looked up.

Before us stood a tall and handsome dark-bearded man, in a semi-clerical garb, which, however, was sadly soiled with mud and blood, and very much torn in several places. The man was in the prime of life, but the paleness of his face contrasted strangely with the depth of colour in his beard. No wonder he looked wan and weary, for his left arm was in a sling, and there was a wound across one temple, which seemed to have been received but recently.

"Man!" said Jock, rising from his seat, "you've got a sad cloot (knock) there. I hope you felled the chiel that dang you."

"He isn't alive to-day," said the stranger, smiling sadly.

"I have just come from Akwaz," he continued. "Mine has been a remarkable escape. I am safe now, however, and would seek the assistance of your General Outram. I am told he is both brave and gallant."

"Well, sir," said Jock, "I can answer for it, he is baith. Just let him in front of the foe, and a braver man never swung a claymore, so early in the morning; but place him alangside laddies and bairnies, and he is the kindest, mildest lad that ever lived."

"I am glad to hear so good a character of your great General, but an English lady is in great distress at Bagdad. I thought it possible he might help me. With one hundred men, if they could but be spared, I would take in hand to secure her release."

"Pussy, pussy," cried Jock, in some alarm, for I had been wistfully gazing at the new arrival since he began to speak, and now sprang lightly from the soldier's shoulder on to his, and began to sing, and rub my head against his ear.

"Can it be possible?" cried the stranger, taking me down and looking at my mouth. "Ruby and all," he added, as if speaking to himself.

You see, Warlock, that I had known the stranger at a glance. He was the good, kind priest who had nursed my master back to health, when wounded by the bandits in the wild forest.

"Soldier," he said excitedly, "this is Shireen."

"She's nobody else," said Jock. "But wha in a' the warl' are ye, that seems so weel acquaint wi' the dear auld cat?"

But now the stranger had seen my master and the surgeon returning, and hurried off to meet them, I still retaining my place in the priest's arms.

The recognition had been mutual and simultaneous.

"This is indeed a happy meeting," both exclaimed.

Then hand met hand in a hearty shake.

"But you are wounded, my friend. Come, let our good surgeon attend to you at once."

The priest was led to the doctor's tent, and master would not let him speak until he had quaffed some refreshment, and had the ugly wound in the forehead attended to.

"And now I must speak to you at once, and alone," said master's friend.

"I am rejoiced to meet you, and I hope it will all end well. But Beebee and Miss Morgan——"

"Yes, yes. Speak! Tell me the worst."

"They have both been removed, under an escort, from her father's palace, and are prisoners near Bagdad."

"In a prison! Good heavens!"

"No, friend, no. Not in a prison. Their home is a beautiful villa on the outskirts of Bagdad. Their gaolers are women and eunuchs."

"And the father?"

"It is the father who has done this, and at the conclusion of the war, or it may be before it, Beebee will be removed to the Shah's palace, and Miss Morgan will be made a slave, if no worse fate befall her. I have escaped and come to tell the tale. It seems to me providential that I have found you."

"It would appear so; but I am indeed in great distress of mind. We cannot, I know, spare a man, for an expedition is just on the eve of starting up the river Karoon to Akwaz. The enemy are falling back in force on that town, and the General wishes to be beforehand with him."

The priest-surgeon put his hand on my master's shoulder.

"Do not be afraid," he said, pointing with a finger skywards. "There is One who rules all things for good. Trust Him. Be patient. All will yet be well."

"Pray Heaven your words may soon come true!"

CHAPTER XXI.

"HAVE HEART AND HOPE, MY FRIEND."

AR away up the river Karoon, my children, lies the city of Akwaz, and it was for this place our three little gunboats, the *Comet*, the *Planet*, and the *Assyria*, now started.

But for the anxiety that I could not help noticing was depicted on my dear master's face, this expedition would have been altogether as nice as a picnic.

We—my master, the priest, Jock and I—went in the *Comet*, with one hundred Highlanders.

Our whole force did not amount to much over three hundred men, and yet with this little mite of an army we were going to attack a town, the size and strength of which we were not even sure of.

I, however, felt no fear, because I heard master say that whatever men dare, they can do.

Well, in due time we reached the town, and we landed, attacked and captured it.

Persians are not cowards. They can fight well, and this army of about nine thousand men would, doubtless, soon have destroyed our bold little force, had it not been so arranged as to look like three invading armies.

Then, of course, we had the support of the gunboats, and, as master said, it was but right to give the Persian general his due. He must have thought that our troops were but the advance-guard of General Outram's whole force. And so he and his army ran away.

" Did much fur fly, Shireen ? " asked Cracker.

Not much, said Shireen. You see, Cracker, we didn't get so near to the enemy as you d d to the butcher's dog that day you saved life, else brave Jock MacNab and master would have made plenty of fur fly.

From the river, the town of Akwaz and the broad sheet of water, with its beautiful wooded islands, and the wild and rugged mountains far behind, formed a scene which was lovely in the extreme.

On the evening after the day on which our gallant force had routed the enemy, and captured the town with all their stores, the priest and my master sat long on deck, talking of the past. I sit on the priest's knee. There was a calm or repose about this man that to me was very delightful, and as he smoothed me while he talked to master, I purred and sang with my eyes half closed.

I was not asleep, however, and I could hear every word they said.

I noticed, too, that this good priest spoke ne'er a word about himself, or his own affairs. He seemed to interest himself in master and in him only. This I thought was very unselfish and considerate of him. It was kind of him, too, to keep master and me company at all, for he was still very weak from his wounds, and a less brave-hearted man would have been confined to his hammo k.

At last we got up steam and departed for the camp

at Mohammerah, and not only our General Sir James Outram, but all our soldier and sailor companions-in-arms were rejoiced to see us, and hailed us as the heroes of Akwaz, which we undoubtedly were, despite the fact that we had suffered but little loss.

But that same day news came which delighted some of us, but grievously disappointed most.

Peace had been proclaimed, and we were to fight no more. This was looked upon by our brave soldiers as a downright shame. Just as the campaign was opening out so hopefully, and there was every prospect that we would, in course of time, conquer the whole of Persia.

But two of our number were very glad of the news, and these were that dear, big priest, and my own beloved master.

They went out together at sunset to talk matters over, as they wandered slowly up and down among the shady date trees. Jock McNab accompanied them at a little distance, and I trotted quietly between the two.

At last they sat down at a spot which afforded them a beautiful view of the river.

"War is a terrible thing, my friend," began the priest. "Are you not glad that peace is concluded?"

"War is, as you say, a terrible thing," replied my soldier-master; "yet I fear we redcoats like it. You see, we all look forward to honour and glory. Every private carries a marshal's baton in his knapsack, figuratively speaking, and yet, for one reason, I am glad this war is over."

"Ah! I knew," said the priest smiling, "that I should soon reach down to that which is next your heart."

"How true and good you are!" said Edgar.

"And do you know what I have done?" continued the priest. "What I have dared to do?"

My master turned quickly round to him.

" You have been to see the General!" he said quickly.

" Indeed I have.'

" And you have told him all the story?"

" I have told him almost all."

" And he——'

" He is going to help us."

" Heaven bless you, dear friend, all your life."

Edgar extended his hand, which the priest shook right cordially.

"Now, you know," the priest said, " I had to tell the General that you were interested indirectly in this affair, and then he at once told me that you and I could go to Bagdad in the *Comet*, which was going there on state business. That he would gladly give an asylum and all assistance to the English lady, Miss Morgan, and to her maid, if she had one, no matter whether she were English or not. Then he shook hands with me and told me to go and talk the whole matter over with you."

My master sat thoughtfully looking at the river for a time, then he turned once more to the priest.

"I can see exactly how the land lies," he said smiling. " How good and thoughtful of the General."

" Yes, he is our friend."

" His horror," added the priest, " at the villainy displayed by a father, who would sell his young and beautiful daughter to the Shah against her will, was plainly discoverable in the manner in which he stamped his foot, and cried, 'Scandalous! Shameful!'"

"And the allusion to the maid——" began Edgar.

"That, you know," said the priest, "is left for you and for me to interpret, as best we may. Miss Morgan must have a maid, must she not?"

"Certainly. Every English lady must have a maid," said my master, smiling a happy smile.

"And it wouldn't do, would it, for the English General to be implicated in the abduction of a Persian noble's daughter?"

"No, certainly not."

"And so you see that——"

"Yes, yes, I see," cried master, laughing right heartily now. "Beebee must, for the time being, become Miss Morgan's lady's-maid. Ha! ha! ha! It is droll."

"Yes, it is droll."

But then master's face fell.

"Ah! my dearest friend," he said, "we may, after all, be counting our chickens before they are hatched."

"Nay, nay, nay," cried the priest. "I have set my heart upon having this strange adventure end well, and end well it must and shall."

"Unless——"

"I know what you would say, captain. Unless Beebee has already been taken off. But I do not think this is at all likely. They do not do things very rapidly in Persia. They are a calm, contemplative kind of people. But, nevertheless, Beebee is doomed to a fate too horrible to think of if we do not rescue her."

"Do you think," said Edgar eagerly, "it will be very, *very* difficult?"

"I do think it will be somewhat difficult. But have heart and hope, my friend. Let me recall to you a motto that I have heard from your own lips."

" And that is ? "

" ' Whate'er a man dares he can do.' "

"And now," said Shireen, "I am going to reserve the last part of my story till we meet again, for, Cracker, your folks must think you are lost, and I can see that the cockatoo yonder is standing on one foot and half asleep."

"Cockie wants to go to bed," cried Uncle Ben's pet, arousing himself, and lifting his great white, yellow-lined wings as if he would fly.

"As for me," said Cracker, "I'd sit and hear you talk all night, you bet."

"And so would I," said Warlock.

"The more I see and learn of cats," continued Cracker, "the more I respects them like, and I don't care a rat's tail what the other dogs say about me. There's that butcher's rag of a bull-terrier, for instance, goin' and tellin' the whole village that I'm often seen in cats' company, and that I'm half a cat myself. Well, I says, says I, I might be something worse. But, bless you, Shireen, next time I meets he, I'm going to let him out."

"I wouldn't kill him quite," said Shireen.

"Oh, no. I'll just shake him like. They kind o' dogs can be killed over and over again, and don't take much hurt. Besides, you know," he added knowingly, "it will teach the varmint manners."

"I say, you know," said Warlock, "I think the quarrel with the butcher's cur should be mine."

"Nonsense, Warlock, he would swallow you up."

"Ah! you don't know how much fight there is in me when I'm fairly angered. Well, I keep company with Tabby here. We hunt together, don't we, Tab?"

"That we do."

"And fish together. So just let that butcher's dog come across me."

"Tse, tse, tse!" said the starling, admiringly. The chameleon simply warmed his other hand before the fire.

I'm not sure, that as far as that goes, Chammy wasn't the wisest in that group of friends. Catch Chammy fighting! He would take a hundred years to make up his mind to do it, and then he wouldn't.

"By-the-bye," said Shireen, "though human folk will have it that dogs and cats don't agree, there is plenty of true stories told by naturalists to prove that when a dog and a cat, indeed, I might say, any dog and any cat are brought up together, they agree like lambs upon a lea. They will wander about together just as Warlock and Tabby do. Eat out of the same dish without quarrelling, and sleep together on the same mat at night.

"I see," added Shireen, "that master and Uncle Ben haven't quite finished their game yet, so while we wait I may as well tell you a little story about cat and dog life. It is mentioned and authenticated in a book called 'Friends in Fur.' " *

This story is told of a cat called the "Czar," and a doggie whose name was "Whiskey." And it is doubly *a propos* because, like Warlock yonder, Whiskey was a Scotch terrier, and he lived in a country village far away in the north of bonnie Scotland. In the same house dwelt

* Same author.

the Czar, a splendid, large, rough-haired cat, who, it
was said, had been imported from Russia—hence his
name.*

No two animals in the world could have loved each other
more dearly and devotedly than did the Czar and his little
wise companion, Whiskey.

Whiskey, I need hardly tell you, Cracker, was like
Warlock there, the gamest of the game, but of course
he never showed his teeth to the Czar. They took their
meals from the same dish, only Whiskey seemed to have
compacted to have all the bones. They were also constantly together, all day long, except when Whiskey's
duty to his master called him afield, and at night they

---

* My friend, Harrison Weir, to whom I am indebted for the speaking illustrations contained in this book, once owned a cat of this breed, and a very
handsome cat it must have been. He speaks of it thus in his book called
"Our Cats," page 30 : "The mane, or frill, was very large, long, and dense,
and more of a woolly texture, with coarse short hairs among it , the colour
was a dark tabby. The eyes were large and prominent, of a bright orange,
slightly tinted with green ; the ears large by comparison, with small tufts full
of long woolly hair ; the limbs stout and short, the tail being very dissimilar,
as it was short, very woolly and thickly tipped with hair, the same length
from base to tip, and much resembled in form that of the British wild cat. Its
motion was not so agile as that of other cats, nor did it apparently care for
warmth, as it liked being out of doors in the coldest weather. Another peculiarity being that it seemed to care little in the way of watching birds for food,
neither were its habits like those of the short-haired cats that were its companions.

"It attached itself to no person, as was the case with some of the others,
but curiously took a particular fancy to one of my short-haired silver tabbies ;
the two appeared always together. In front of the fire they sat side by side.
If one left the room the other followed. Adown the garden paths they were
still companions ; and at night they slept in the same box ; they drank milk
from the same saucer, and fed from the same plate, and, in fact, only seemed
to exist for each other. In all my experience I never saw a more devoted
couple."

shared the selfsame bed ; the Czar often taking Whiskey in his arms because he appeared to be the biggest. I'm not sure, indeed, that the Czar did not awaken Whiskey when that little gentleman took the nightmare. Be this as it may, they were, altogether, as loving as loving could be.

And once or twice a week this kindly couple used to go out hunting together.

" Just like Warlock and me," said Tabby.

Yes, said Shireen, and they cared nothing for game laws, and took no heed of the keepers, except to hide or run from them ; for this cat and dog were a law unto themselves apparently.

On their hunting expeditions they used to go out together in the morning, and after spending all the long day in the woods and wilds, they invariably came home before dark.

This coming home before nightfall was no doubt a suggestion of Whiskey's, for a dog can neither see so well in the dark as a cat, nor can his constitution so easily withstand the dews of night. But the very fact of the Czar's consenting to keep early hours to please his Scottish friend, is another proof of how dearly he must have loved him.

And almost every night these sons of Nimrod brought home with them some trophy from the hunting-ground. Sometimes it was a rabbit, more often a bird—if the latter, Whiskey generally had the honour of carrying it, and very proud was he of the distinction ; if a small rabbit, the Czar bore the burden.

And so things went on till one mournful night, when Whiskey returned later than usual and all alone. He came into the house, but lay down on the mat near the door, and from that he would not budge an inch. He refused his porridge and all consolation, and lay there in a nervous

WHISKEY AND CZAR.

P

and acutely listening attitude, starting up whenever he heard the slightest sound outside.

His mistress at last went to bed and left him.

It must have been long past midnight when Whiskey came dashing into his mistress's bedroom, knocking over a chair in his excitement, and barking wildly as he rushed hither and thither.

When his mistress got up at last poor little Whiskey preceded her to the door, barking again and looking anxious and excited.

Outside a pitiful mew was heard, and as soon as the lady opened the door in rushed the Czar on three legs. He had left one foot in a horrid trap.

And now nothing could exceed the kindness of the dog towards his wounded companion and playmate. He threw himself down on the rug beside her, whining and crying with very grief, and gently licked the bleeding stump where the cat himself had gnawed it off to save his life.

And every day for weeks did Whiskey apply hot fomentations with his soft wee tongue to pussy's leg, until at last it was completely healed.

But they had no more romping together in fields and woods, for the Czar's hunting-days were over—in this world at all events.

*   *   *

"Cornered at last," cried Uncle Ben, laughing, as he looked at the chess-board. "No, you haven't a move. Ho! ho! Well, I've had my revenge."

"And I," said the Colonel, "shall have mine another evening."

"Right you are.   Now, good-bye, Lizzie and Tom.
Come, Cracker, old dog, you go my way, don't you?"

So good-nights were said, and hands were shaken, and
off went Uncle Ben and his cockatoo adown the road
towards his bungalow, where his man Pedro was waiting
to place before him his frugal supper.

CHAPTER XXII.

HE school stood quite in the suburbs of the little village—the girls' school I mean—and there was nothing very unusual about it. Year in and year out, with certainly no more holidays than they deserved, the teachers—orphan girls both—laboured all day long at their duties, and had the satisfaction of knowing that they were well beloved by their sometimes noisy pupils, to whom their wish, however, was always law ; and the children generally made a good show when examination time came round.

It was in here, one hard frosty day, that Shireen dropped on her way down town, to pay her usual round of visits.

She had just left Uncle Ben's bungalow, after a long talk and song with the sailor, and a few words to Cockie, the cockatoo, who, if he did not say very much, was a wonderful mimic, and made many droll motions. He never saw a boy, for example, without going through the movements of using a whip. Perhaps Cockie believed with Solomon, that it was a pity to "spare the rod and spoil the child."

There was a kind of general welcome to Shireen when she entered the school-house ; but, strangely enough, she went straight up to the desk, and paid her compliments to the two teachers before doing anything else.

Then Shireen looked about her from the seat she had taken, namely, a high three-legged stool. She could, from this elevation, see a large number of her little friends, with whom she would hold a little conversation presently. But there was one homely, good-natured face that she missed, and one of the teachers, as if reading her thoughts, stroked her back and head, as she remarked with a smile,

"Emily isn't here to-day, Pussy."

"No," said the other girl. "Emily has been a good girl, and worked hard ; and she has finished her education, and gone home to keep house for her father."

So Shireen did not stop so long to-day in the school as was her wont, for the chief attraction was gone. But she dispensed her favours among her friends freely enough before she went. And they were not all girls, either, whom Shireen regarded affectionately. For though it was a girls' school, there were tiny, wee pests of fair-haired boys there, not an inch bigger, presumably, than the school tongs, and of one or two of these Shireen seemed very fond.

Down the room she trotted at last, however. She was not long in meeting with an adventure, for round the distant corner came Danger, the butcher's bull-terrier. There wasn't a good tree within fifty yards, so Shireen had a race for it. She got up into the sycamore safely, nevertheless. Danger coming in a good second, and stopping to bark savagely up at her.

Shireen raised her back and growled defiance down at him.

Then she taunted him.

"Why don't you come up?" she cried derisively. "Why don't you climb the tree? Because you can't, clever though you think yourself. Fuss! Futt! Wouldn't I make the fur fly out of you if you did come up. And wouldn't I carve my name on your nose, just. Go home! Go home, you ugly brute. Mind, you'll catch it when Cracker meets you. Oh, he'll give it to you properly next time."

The dog trotted off at last, and then Shireen came slowly down.

She meant to-day to pay all her other visits before going to Emily's, because then she would have longer time to stay with her. So she went first to see Jeannie Lynch, at her mother's tiny earthen-floored cottage. Jeannie's mother was an invalid, and would never be better. But she could just sit by the fire in her high-backed chair, and do knitting, while Jeannie attended to the housewifery. Shireen found the girl busy washing up the dinner things, and singing low to herself. But there was a subdued, chastened kind of a look on her pretty face, which was habitual to it, for Jeannie was lame, and, I'm sorry to say, the village children teased her and called "Box-foot" after her. So even when she went out to do shopping for her mother, she limped along the street, looking fifty years of age, instead of the eleven summers that made up the sum total of her existence hitherto. She looked, indeed, as if she owed people an apology for her somewhat ungainly appearance.

Shireen loved her, nevertheless, and she loved Shireen, and it wasn't for sake of the drop of milk Jeannie always put down for her, nor in the hope of catching the mouse that nibbled paper in the cupboard, that pussy always stopped at least an hour at this humble dwelling.

But she had to go at last, because she must see Mr. Burn-the-wind, and also little Alec Dewsbury. Alec was one of the afflicted. At school one day, when quite a tiny lad, he had somehow injured his spine, and on a small, stretcher-bed he had lain helpless for years. Often in summer he lay out in the garden under the tree's green shade, where he could hear the birds sing, and look up at the sailing clouds, with the rifts of blue between ; and higher still in imagination, far, far away beyond the blue, where they told him God and angels dwell, though God was everywhere. In winter his stretcher stood in a cosy corner of his cottage home ; and kind people brought him books and papers to read. But Alec's pale face always lit up with joy when Shireen came in, for he had no pet of his own.

" I wonder," he said to his mother one day, "if cats go to heaven ? Oh, surely they do," he added, before she could answer. "I'm certain all good and beautiful creatures go there. Besides, mother, we know there are cows and bees there."

"What put that in your head, lammie ?"

"Because it's a land flowing with milk and honey, you know ; so there must be cows and bees there."

Alec was a very, very old boy for his years.

The blacksmith, on this particular day, was in very fine form, and making the sparks fly in golden horizontal showers just as Shireen trotted in to say "good-day." He had four ragamuffins of rosy-faced children, perched high on a bench, with their legs dangling in the air, to whom he was relating an old-fashioned fairy tale, which made them laugh at one moment, and stare with wonder and astonishment the next. Shireen knew all four children, so she jumped up, and seated herself beside the smallest, a mite of a girl, who at once declared to the others that pussy loved her "bestest of all."

Then the blacksmith smoothed Shireen with the back of his hand, because it was the only unsoiled portion of that horny fist of his, and then he went on with his story.

While they were all listening, Lizzie and Tom ran in. Tom had his skates slung over his shoulder ; and his sister carried a basket, which contained many a dainty, and many a little luxury for the aged and the indigent sick.

Like pussy herself, Lizzie and Tom were always welcome, whether they had a basket or not ; because, even when they did not bring little gifts of jelly, or beef-tea, or books, or snuff and tobacco, they brought smiles, and the sunshine of their innocent and winsome ways.

But to-day, neither Lizzie nor Tom stayed long with Burn-the-wind, because the former had her basket to lighten and hearts to lighten thereby, and because Tom noticed there was no horse to be shod at present, and he knew that the ice on the mill-pond was inches thick.

"Oh, dear! Oh, dear!" cried Lizzie, as they got nearer to the top of the street. "Something surely has happened. Look, Tom, at the lot of the people, and they are carrying somebody. Oh, Tom, it is Emily, I know and feel sure."

Yes, it was Emily.

Poor girl! Only the day before, she had returned from school for good. She was going to settle down now, she told everyone of her intimate friends, laughing gleefully. She was going to do her father's little house-keeping ; and poor old dad, as she called him, would in future have many a comfort he had missed since mother died.

And baby, too, would not be so much neglected, and could be taken out every forenoon, after father had gone back to work.

There was a bit of garden, too, behind the humble cottage, with a nice grass plot in the centre ; there, in spring and summer, the daisies grew, and the yellow celandines.

Bobby, her infant brother, could roll on the grass when it was dry and fine, while she did the gardening all around. And this would be so delightful, because then she would never want a flower to place on mother's grave.

So you will observe, dear reader, that it was all beautifully arranged.

Alas! and alas! If I were writing an altogether imaginary story, the somewhat sad and sombre ending to this chapter would be altered. But there is far more of truth in my story than anyone will ever know.

That day then, when Emily took her little brother out in his far from elegant perambulator, she heard the sound of a band. A wild-beast show was stationed on the village green it seemed, and there was a triumphal procession through the streets of the little town. Poor Emily stood aside to see it pass, for, despite the fact that children would be admitted to the great marquee for half-price, this procession was the only part of the show she would see. But she marvelled much at the lordly ungainliness of the elephants ; at the queer, old-fashioned visages of the camels, and at the wisdom of the piebald pony, and the wit of the immortal clown who rode him, who had appeared—didn't the bills tell her so?—before every respectable crowned head in Europe. But she stood agape with astonishment when she saw the beautiful and airily dressed "Lion Queen," perched high on top of her gilded carriage.

Then the procession passed on, and Emily resumed her journey with the perambulator. Not far up the street she remembered that she wanted some tobacco for her father, and that she had passed the shop. She left the perambulator where it was for a few minutes, till she should run back and make the little purchase.

As she stood at the counter she heard the quick rattle of wheels, and a noise of galloping hoofs, and then the shout of "Horse ran off!" fell upon her ear.

"Oh, the baby!" cried Emily, and dashed out of the shop.

The perambulator, with the child in it, laughing and blinking in the sunshine, stood right in the track of danger.

But Emily, heedless of everything except the desire to save her brother, rushed on towards it. Nearer and nearer came the horse. People shrieked as they saw the girl at the perambulator.

One push sent it clear away from under the very hoofs of the fear-maddened horse. Next moment, Emily herself was down.

Then the sorrowful procession.

Two hours after Lizzie and Tom had seen Emily borne by kind and loving hands into the humble cottage that had been her home, the doctor came out.

He shook his head sadly.

"Go home, my friends," he said, "it is all over."

He jumped into his carriage and was driven away. But tears trickled down the cheeks of men in that little crowd ; faces were buried in aprons, and women wept aloud.

The grief of poor Emily's father was something to see and remember for ever and a day. I am not going to attempt to describe it. He was a good man, and a Christian ; yet, not that night, nor for many nights and days, was he able to see the light, and to say from his heart: "The Lord gave, and the Lord has taken away, blessed be His name."

                                                        ✻

As to Shireen—I must tell you about her. She never left the cottage while Emily's poor little body lay there ; and had you entered the house the night before the funeral, you would have seen the poor father sitting by his half out fire, absorbed in grief, and Shireen upon the coffin-lid.

In the cat's face sorrow, intense sorrow, predominated ; but there was also a touch of anger also. Why was her favourite here in this dark box ? What had they done to her ? Who had done it ?

Ah ! there was a mystery somewhere, which this little feline playmate and friend of the deceased girl failed to fathom. Can we, in our wisdom ? Alas, no !

LITTLE EMILY'S CHIEF MOURNER.

CHAPTER XXIII.

INTER had passed and gone. It had fled far away to Norland hills, and spring reigned in its stead.

Sweet-voiced, hopeful spring! Spring, that is always so full of love and joy. Spring, with the balmy wind that whispers softly through the woods and groves, mingling its voice with the purling song of the brooklet and rill, sighing over fields of waving corn, and wooing the odours from a thousand wild flowers. Spring, with its chorus of joy-birds, whose melodies ring out from every woodland, every thicket and grove, till all the green earth seems to lift up its voice in a chorus of gladness and mirth. Sweet-voiced, hopeful spring, the poet's one season of all the seasons of the year.

The old castle lawn was beautiful again, green with verdure and starred over with daisies, and out there now Lizzie and Tom were able to play and gambol once more, where Uncle Ben, with his cockatoo, and the Colonel used to sit there in their good straw chairs, smoke their pipes, and talk together of the days of auld lang syne.

Out on this lawn on one particularly blue-skied sunny

afternoon, Shireen and her friends were assembled, Warlock looking as wise as ever, Vee-Vee as gentle and loving,
and Cracker, with his droll, rough, kindly face, all willing
to please.

"Shireen," said Cracker, "we haven't heard you speak
for a long time."

Shireen paused in the middle of the operation of face-
washing and sat on her mat for a moment or two, with her
paw raised thoughtfully in front of her.

"You see," she said at last, "it takes some time for grief
like what I suffered for poor Emily to die away. Oh,
mine isn't gone even yet, and somehow I feel older since
they took and buried my girl friend. But this is not
going to prevent me from concluding my story, and
I'm sure I ought to be glad to see you all around me
on this lovely afternoon, and to know that we are all alive
and well."

"Let me see, where did I leave off in my story about
my master and Beebee?"

"Oh, I remember," cried Warlock. "You and your
master were about to start on a long journey up the great
river to a town called—what was it called though?"

"Bagdad!" cried Shireen. "I have it all now. Yes,
and the kind good-natured priest was going with us."

Well, my children, Bagdad, you know, is far away
to the north, and high up the winding Tigris. Oh, that
river does wind to be sure, in and out, out and in, and
sometimes it really flows north when it might be saving
time by keeping on towards the sunny south, or the golden
east. But I dare say, after all, the river knows best, and
is in no great hurry to leave this lovely land.

Not all lovely is it, though, for even at the places

where the river winds the most, the banks are low and wide, stretching afar on each side, and bounded by rising hills, with here and there a tuft of palm trees.

But at other places the river goes hurrying on rapidly, as in terror and dread of the very wildness of the scenery, tall beetling cliffs, impassable jungles and bare-scalped rocks, rising brown above the greenery of storm-rent woods and forests. This is the home of many a strange and beautiful bird, the resort of many a savage beast.

" Grand opening for sport, Shireen," said Cracker.

" Ah, Cracker, you are strong and big and brave, and your teeth are like daggers of ivory, but short indeed would your existence be if you attempted sport in this lovely wilderness. There are beasts herein, Cracker, one touch from the paws of which would end all your joys and troubles as well."

" I'm not going there then, Shireen. Yorkshire or Scotland is good enough for me, and I'd as soon tackle a Bingley badger as a Bagdad tiger, you bet."

On and on went our little vessel, Chammy, up the waters of the broad, deep river.

" How happy I should be to-day," I heard my master remark to the priest, " if it were not for this ever-abiding anxiety."

He put one hand upon his heart as he spoke.

" We must trust to Providence and do our best," replied the priest with a smile. " You are not giving way to despair, are you, my friend ? "

" No, my best of friends. But I cannot help feeling within me a strange comminglement of hope and doubt, of joy and fear. Oh, Antonio, if anything happens to that dear child, I shall not want to live one single hour longer. I should——"

Q

"Hush! hush! *mon ami*, I feel certain it will all come right."

My master grasped his hand.

"How much I admire your repose, your calmness, and your perfect trust in Providence."

* * * *

Most of the officers had now congregated round the bows, one or two only being on the little bridge, for we were within but a few miles of the strange quaint city of Bagdad. But what a lovely picture the river and its banks now made! Here was many a beautiful house and charming villa, in whose gardens or lawns lovely children were playing. There were flowers everywhere, and everywhere were orchards all in bloom, pink, crimson, and snow-white.

The river was very rapid here indeed, so our progress was slow; but except my master, no one on board I believe would have cared to have it any quicker.

He was standing astern, near the wheel, gazing dreamily into the water, when the priest advancing, led him aside. Then he pointed to a strange-looking building on a low hill, surrounded by waving woods. It seemed partly a villa and partly a fort.

"They are there!" said the priest. "Miss Morgan and her maid."

I could see the colour come and go on my dear master's face, and really felt sorry for him at that moment.

"Pray Heaven," he said, "we are not too late, Antonio."

"Better now," said Antonio, "leave all to me. This is a matter of life and death. If I keep calm and cool my head will be clear and I shall succeed. If I lose my presence of mind for one moment, Miss Morgan and her maid may——"

"What?"

"Die."

"Antonio!" said my master, "I leave all to you. I trust you thoroughly."

Our little steamboat was now rapidly getting near to Bagdad, the city of Kaliphs, and all at once we rounded a bank, and there burst upon our gaze a scene which is as impressive as any, my children, I have ever witnessed.

Perhaps our sudden appearance caused as much astonishment to the people of Bagdad as their strange city caused to us. For very quickly, before indeed we had thought of casting anchor, boats began to crowd shyly round us; boats strange in shape, boats laden with strange passengers and gaily-dressed Turkish men and women, whose veils scarce concealed their beauty, boats flitting hither and thither on trade or pleasure bent, and high up the stream a wonderful bridge built of boats.

The city itself, along the side of the river, seemed a city of palaces, of domes and minarets, of cupolas and towers. There was beauty and brightness everywhere, and the tall waving palm-trees, that shot upwards their green-fringed tops against the blue sky and fleecy clouds, lent to the whole scene additional charm.

But anchor was let go at last, right in front of the charmingly-kept gardens of the British Consul, and master, with Antonio and other officers, went on shore to visit him.

That night the Consul himself came off to our little ship, and master confided to him—for he was a kindly man —the whole story of Beebee, and sought his advice.

This was willingly given.

"It seems strange, however," said Mr. Wilson, the consul, "that she should have been sent to Bagdad."

"This was no doubt for safety," said Antonio, "although the visit was said to have been recommended by the Persian doctor for health's sake, and she is as strictly guarded here as she would be in her own country."

"Well," said Mr. Wilson, "any assistance that is in my power to give you, you may depend upon. Meanwhile, I think that your plan of getting Miss Morgan and her maid away by stealth affords the best chance for the safety and perhaps the lives of both."

Two days after this all was arranged, and Antonio, dressed as a travelling merchant of Persia, and accompanied by myself, dropped down stream in a hired boat.

But little did I know then the important part I was to play in the delivery of my poor mistress from the fate that threatened her.

CHAPTER XXIV.

H! Miss Morgan," cried Beebee. "How is this all to end?"

My mistress was sitting on the balcony of the room when she made this remark, and Miss Morgan, her English governess, was by her side.

The window overlooked the orchards, that went sweeping down towards the banks of the swift-flowing Tigris; and on the far horizon, high above a cloudland of trees, rose here and there the painted cupolas and gilded minarets of the great city of Bagdad itself.

"I hardly know yet, my dear child, how it will end. I have prayed, Beebee, prayed long and earnestly, and I have hope, and for some reason or another which I cannot explain, I associate the passing of that British steamer with our deliverance."

"And I, too, have prayed to the Christian God; but somehow He gives me not the hope that He seems to give to you. Suppose," she added, "we could escape to Bagdad, and reach your British ship, would she give us shelter?"

"As a last resort I may counsel this, Beebee, mine; but, ah! think of the risk. The chance of discovery is very great, and you know what discovery means."

"Yes," sighed Beebee, "it means, to me at all events, death, and a bed beneath yon dark flowing river. And yet I feel I should like to take the risk, dear teacher. In a few days, at most, we shall be sent back to our own home, for the peace has come. Then, oh, dear Miss Morgan, it will be too late."

"See how lovely the sunset is," she added, with a sigh, "and listen, teacher, to the song of those happy birds. Ah! every creature is happy that is free. I—I—oh, teacher, I am the veriest slave!"

Poor Beebee leant her head on the shoulder of her companion, and burst into tears.

It was at this very moment, my children, that I, led by some unerring instinct that I cannot even describe to you, crept through the orchard and leapt upon the balcony with a joyful cry.

Antonio had brought me within two hundred yards of the house.

"Your mistress is not far off, Shireen," he said; "go, seek her."

I had sought her. I had found her. Oh, happy hour; but for a time neither she nor Miss Morgan knew me.

Beebee looked up when I came in, her face still streaming with tears.

I sang aloud, and rubbed my head and back against her; and at last a light seemed suddenly to dawn upon her. She stared at me for a moment almost in fright, and superstitiously. Then gradually a smile crept around her lips and eyes.

"Oh, teacher!" she cried. "Can it be possible? Take her up, quick, and look for the ruby."

"Yes, yes, I am right," she added quickly, as Miss

Morgan exposed my gum for a moment, and showed the gem set fast in my tooth. "Oh, I was sure of it!"

And then I was held fast to Beebee's beating heart.

Miss Morgan was looking strangely puzzled. She was thinking.

"I cannot understand," she said, at last. "What can it possibly mean, Beebee? And how *could* Shireen have come here?"

"You cannot understand," cried Beebee gladly. "Oh, but I do. They tell us love is blind. It is false. For I can see; I can see it all. My prince is near at hand, and soon he will come. He is, indeed, he must be in that very ship that passed on up the river to Bagdad."

Miss Morgan's eyes now began to gladden with joy.

"What you say must be true," she said. "And deliverance is at hand. We have but to wait."

I felt happier now than ever I had done in my life before. Night fell soon; and I retired with my dear mistress into the luxuriously-furnished apartment, just as slaves began to light the lamps.

They took no notice of the strange pussy.

By-and-bye, the tall, black, fierce-eyed eunuch himself came in, with boys bearing refreshments. But even he did not know me. He had not Beebee's eyes of love.

Beebee talked to him to-night pleasantly too. She even teased him a little, as she used to do when more of a child.

He looked pleased, happy even. He seemed to love his mistress; and yet, this man, at the bidding of his master, Beebee's father, would have thrust her shrieking into a sack, and cast her into the Tigris, whose dark waters close, every month, over many a lovely female form, doomed to death by their heartless husbands.

"How long now," she asked the eunuch "before we return to our own lovely Persian home? Oh, I am sick of Bagdad."

"But two, three days, then I have the order."

"Ah!" he added, "my little bird-mistress will rejoice when at last the Shah sends for her!"

Beebee clapped her little hands.

"Indeed, indeed, I shall be joyful," she said, "when the day of my deliverance comes."

I slept that night in Beebee's apartment; but the whole of next forenoon wore away and nothing unusual occurred, and I began to notice that sadness was once more stealing over the face of my young mistress.

But when it was once more close upon sunset, the eunuch glided silently up to the window of the balcony, on which Beebee sat, with Miss Morgan and me.

"Would the ladies be amused?" he asked. "A Persian merchant, with a box of jewellery and many fine things, would like to spread his wares at their feet?"

A quick glance passed betwixt Miss Morgan and Beebee, and the latter smiled and nodded assent.

In a few minutes more, Antonio, the priest, prostrated himself on the mosaic, before the now veiled ladies; but was told he might arise and show his wares.

He lost no time in doing so, and Beebee lifted up her hands and laughed with delight. For here were gems and jewels, rich and rare; dresses of every description, and toys of curious workmanship.

"Oh, Jazr!" she cried to the eunuch. "You have been always so good and kind to me, and I may not again have such an opportunity of presenting you with a gift. Wear, for my sake, Jazr, this chain of gold, and think of me when I am far away, as I soon shall be, you know."

The eunuch was profuse in his thanks.

"And now," added Beebee, "go, good Jazr, and bring me my two favourite female slaves. You have to-day made Beebee happy, and she will show her joy by giving them also gifts of value."

Next moment Jazr was gone.

Though he was not absent from the room a minute, for he had but to go a little way along the passage and clap his hands, there was time for a few words to pass between Beebee and Antonio.

"You know me?" he said in English.

"Yes, yes," in a quick whisper.

"Buy this gold watch as a gift for Miss Morgan, and open it when alone. Buy, also, this large parcel of silk. It contains all you will require to insure your safety."

In half an. hour more, Antonio, the Persian merchant, was gone, and the whole house and garden had resumed their usual quiet.

Hours passed away. Then over all the country fell the silence of the night, scarce broken even by the song of birds in the orchards and groves.

The window of Beebee's sleeping apartment was fully thirty feet above ground ; but it overlooked a wild piece of jungle or woody thicket, into which, if anyone could drop, he or she would be beyond the walls of this prison villa, and presumably free.

Oh, children, continued Shireen, after a brief pause. I am very old now, but were I to live as long again, I should not forget the anxiety and terror of the hour that succeeded midnight.

In Beebee's apartment slept two girl slaves, and on a mat outside the door, the red-eyed eunuch, Jazr, himself.

There was a dim light in the room, that came from a little taper floating in a glass of oil. That was all; and it just served to render things dimly visible.

Quick though my hearing was, I heard no footstep when Miss Morgan stood beside Beebee's couch, and lightly touched her shoulder. She was dressed in a long dark cloak of some kind, the hood of which was over her head.

One finger was on her lip, as if to counsel silence and caution. But there was no need of this, for Beebee had been awake for some time, and knew now that the hour of action had come.

She got up at once, but slowly, cautiously.

My heart beat high with dread at that moment, for there was the sound of talking outside the door. Miss Morgan held up a finger, and both girls paused, waited and listened.

It had been but the eunuch talking in his sleep, for he soon resumed his heavy breathing, and as far as he was concerned, all seemed safe for the time being. Miss Morgan now stepped across to the place where the two little slave-maids lay, and bent for a moment over them. Both were sleeping soundly, and she drew a breath of relief.

Then she went directly to the window, followed by Beebee and myself. It was an open jalousie, and to a hook in the wall I noticed that a thin ladder of silken ropes had been attached and flung over.

This was the most trying moment.

By the taper's pale glimmer I noticed that my dear young mistress was white with fear.

Miss Morgan now took me on her shoulder, and next moment swung herself over the window-sill, descending, it appeared to me, to certain death in the awful darkness.

When her head was level with the sill, she beckoned to Beebee.

"When I g've the signal," she whispered, "hesitate not a moment, but speed downwards. Remember, it is for freedom, and for life itself; and, Beebee, for your prince."

How brave Miss Morgan was!

In two minutes' time, though it seemed to me it was an hour, we had reached the ground. Then Miss Morgan held fast the end of the silken ladder, and gave the signal.

There was no response!

What a fearful moment that was! Surely my mistress had fainted, or had the slaves awakened and held her?

I glanced upwards. Oh, joy! Against the dim, grey light above the trees, and against our prison wall, something dark was visible. And descending too.

It must be; it *was*, Beebee.

But see; she is still ten feet at least above the ground, when from the window, high above, comes a piercing shriek.

The slaves have awakened and given the alarm.

Beebee has paused in her descent. She is petrified with fear.

Next moment she lets go her hold and falls.

Ah! but inanimate though she be, for she has fainted, she is safe. Strong arms have caught her; and next moment, while the great bell of our prison villa clangs forth from the turret its iron notes of alarm, we dash into the deepest, darkest part of the wood, guided by Antonio, the priest, who is carrying Beebee, and in a few minutes more are close by the river's brink.

Clang—clang—clang, goes the dreadful bell!

There is not a moment to lose. Lights are already springing up here and there, by the side of the dark stream. A boat is now liable to be intercepted or even fired upon.

Antonio steps lightly into the skiff. Miss Morgan—I still clinging to her shoulder—quickly follows, and takes Beebee, still insensible, from his arms.

One light push, one touch of the oars, and we are off and away into mid-stream, and soon speeding down the dark river to freedom and to safety.

I think that even Cracker himself drew his breath more freely now that Shireen had reached this part of the story. There could not be much more of it. Only they all wanted to hear the very, very end. So they waited in silence.

The forest would have been searched, said Shireen, everywhere; and everywhere next day, boats would dart up and down the river. But all too late, for we were all safe and sound on board that little British boat, and gaily steaming down the river.

A few weeks after this we reached Bombay, and here, once more, I had to part with Beebee, my mistress; for the terrible Indian Mutiny had broken out, and I and my master had to stay with our regiment; while Miss Morgan and her pupil, with the dear, good priest, Antonio, sailed homewards round the Cape.

Heigho! sighed Shireen. That was a terrible war, and it would take me weeks and weeks to tell you of all I heard and saw. And it was all very, very sad, too.

But dear master gained what he called honour and glory; though for the life of me, my children, I never could see where that came in, or what it meant, but it is something that soldiers and sailors greatly love, and often sigh for.

The longest time has an end, Warlock, and when the horrors of the mutiny were all things of the past, and the sun of peace shedding once more its soft rays over beautiful India, master and I found ourselves sailing back to merrie England.

Yes, Tabby, we sailed in the dear old corvette *Hydra*, and Tom was there—Tom Brandy. Need I say that I was happy?

The first place that master started for, when the ship reached English shores, was his aunt's pretty home in Yorkshire.

Almost the first words he said, when his good old auntie sailed smiling into the room, were,

"Well, my dear aunt, I am so pleased to get back alive and well; but tell me, how is the blackamoor?"

"Oh, your blackamoor," cried his aunt, laughing. She is not far away, nor Miss Morgan either; and she is the dearest, sweetest child on earth. Here she comes!"

Yes, there she came. And never had I seen her look more lovely, more gentle, and good.

Children! a marriage took place sometime after this, and Beebee became the wife of Colonel Edgar Clarkson.

"What!" cried Warlock. "Our master that is now?"

"Yes," said Shireen, nodding.

"And," said Tabby, "Beebee is our mistress?"

"None other."

"Oh, how delightful! How charming!"

"Tsc, tsc, tsc!" said Dick, the starling, and off he flew to Lizzie, who, with her brother Tom, was reclining on the lawn, making gowan* garlands to hang around their favourites' necks.

Dick alighted on Lizzie's head, and at once began to go through the motions of bathing and splashing in the sheen of her bonnie hair.

But Dick's departure seems the signal for the breaking up of the party.   For lo! shades of evening have begun to fall.

> "And in the painted oriel of the West,
>   Whose panes the sunken sun incardines,
>   Like a fair lady at her casement, shines
>   The Evening Star, the star of love and rest."

So "good-nights" are said, and hands are shaken, then slowly homewards to his bungalow, by the pathway under the lindens, swings honest Ben and his cockatoo; while the shadows deepen beneath the trees, and the blackbird trills his last sweet song.

Behind him walks Cracker—a garland of gowans around his neck—all the way to the bungalow gate. Here he stops a moment to receive Ben's friendly farewell pat, then gives his droll old stump of a tail a shake, and trots slowly home alone.

---

* The gowan is the mountain daisy.

THE END.

Selections from Jarrolds' New Books.

POPULAR BOOKS FOR BOYS AND GIRLS.

Uniformly Bound, Small 4to, Cloth Elegant, Price 3/6.

Sable and White. The Autobiography of a Show Dog. By DR. GORDON-STABLES, C.M., R.N. Author of "*Friends in Fur*," "*The Cruise of the 'Snowbird,'*" "*Our Friend the Dog*," &c. Beautifully illustrated by HARRISON WEIR. 2nd Edition.

The Author has for his object the amelioration of the condition of the "Companion and the Friend of Man," performing for the Dog the same kindly office as in "BLACK BEAUTY" has been performed for the Horse.

"This is a very pleasing story by Dr. Stables, who knows so well how to secure the interest of all young readers. It is altogether a splendid gift-book."—*Glasgow Herald.*

"To all boys and girls who cannot reproach themselves with having been unkind to their dumb friends, the book will be both enjoyable and profitable."—*Dundee Advertiser.*

"'Sable and White' purports to be the autobiography of a show dog, and it is enough to say that the text is by Dr. Gordon-Stables, and the illustrations by Mr. Harrison Weir, to indicate that both alike are rich in graphic power and in fidelity to nature."—*Leeds Mercury.*

"Mr. Harrison Weir's illustrations add to the charm of the book, which will delight every boy who loves dogs—that is to say, every well-regulated boy."—*Scottish Leader.*

"The book is a very good one for boys and girls, and there are points in it which even adults could profit by."—*Belfast Evening Telegraph.*

"All lovers of animals will revel in it."—*Newsagent.*

"As a writer for boys Dr. Stables has justly won high fame, and he is, as his readers know, a great lover of animals. Both these characteristics find full play in this his latest work, which will charm the boys while winning their sympathy for the beautiful collie whose adventures it narrates."—*The Christian.*

"The work cannot fail to please young readers for whom it is designed. It has an exceptional charm in the sketches of dogs with which Mr. Harrison Weir has illustrated it, and which add much to its value." – *The Scotsman.*

"This beautifully printed book is just the thing for a present for a boy of ten or thereabouts."—*Nature Notes.*

London: Jarrold and Sons, 10, and 11, Warwick Lane, E.C.

Of all Booksellers and at the Bookstalls.

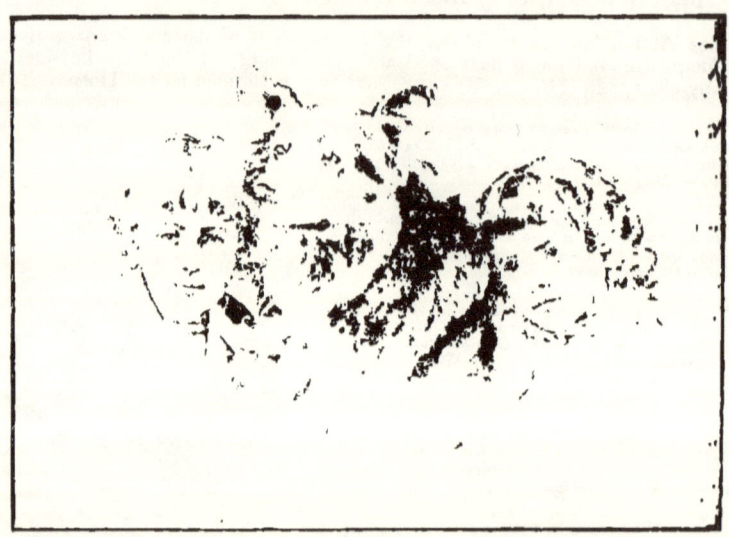

www.ingramcontent.com/pod-product-compliance
Lightning Source LLC
Chambersburg PA
CBHW031423020726

47499CB00005B/1573